SAPLING'S AURORA

SPENCER ROSE

SAPLING'S AURORA

First published in 2023 by Spencer Rose

For more information, email spencer@spencerrosewrites.com

ISBN 978-0-6453613-7-7 (paperback)
ISBN 978-0-6453613-2-2 (digital edition)

2 3 4 5 6 7 8 9 10

Cover Art by Petyr Donat
Cover Design by Sarah Anderson.

spencerrosewrites.com

CONTENTS

ONE

The low oxygen alarm had been blip-blip-blipping for hours. Mila sat in the pilot's chair of the spacecraft, maneuvering a course to the nearest habitable planet. Her knuckles were white on the steering wheel. The engines were off, and we were just using thrusters, gliding through space. We'd used the last of our spare power reserves to fling ourselves across the system using the gravity of one of the larger planets we passed as a slingshot. Mila's plan had been to travel as far as the ship could physically take us, even when we ran out of power and, it seemed, oxygen. The Evo corporation would look for us at ports a day or two from Prema. We'd travelled a week on the ship and then an extra day on thrusters. Now that we were truly at the end of our reserves, we'd picked a planet and set our course.

"Evo knows that this class of ship isn't designed to travel this far without docking at a port," Mila had said yesterday when she'd first switched off the engine, "So they won't be searching for us out here,"

I thought that no one would be searching for our bodies this far out, either.

"We have one hour of oxygen left," Mila reported, reading the blipping indicator.

I sat at the little fold-down table in the galley behind the pilot bay, scanning news alerts on a tablet.

"No news has come through about us," I called.

"Good. The alert Evo has on us must still be for their employees only. We don't want there to be a public manhunt for us." She locked the steering wheel in place and stood up, wincing. Her legs were stiff from the long stretch of sitting and steering the ship manually. Her blue jumpsuit clung to her with sweat patches across her back, and her usually curly hair looked limp against her brow. Her green eyes frowned as she stood, reading the tablet over my shoulder.

"What's this planet?"

"This planet we're heading to is Birumu. It's a farming planet. There is no major spaceport."

"Sounds like a good place to lie low for a few days," she nodded. "We can recharge on the planet and then keep moving,"

We coasted toward the planet, now caught in its gravity. Sitting amidst a scattering of stars, the planet's surface looked brown and blue, with ripples of green light across the clouds. It looked like it had some ocean but was mostly flat landscapes. In space, several satellites were drifting about the planet. Like other satellites I'd seen, they looked like small docking bays stacked with large crates, all in a neat ring.

As I looked at the planet Birumu, I couldn't believe that only two weeks ago, I'd left the forest village I'd always lived in to go on my pilgrimage. Things went downhill rapidly. I'd met Mila and crossed paths with Evo - the corporation now on the hunt for us. Because of something I did. Or something Mila did. We weren't quite sure. We just knew that right now, we needed to run and hide. My stomach had butterflies as we set course for yet another unknown planet.

"You might want to prepare for landing," Mila said, doing a few stretches before resuming her position in the pilot seat.

I headed to the bathroom. I looked as bad as Mila did. My light brown hair was plastered to my face, I had bags under my dark eyes, and my pale skin looked almost transparent in this dimly lit cubicle. I washed my face, tied back my hair, and changed my dress. I still could use an actual shower, but this would do until we recharged the power supply.

The planet loomed over the ship when I returned to the pilot bay.

Mila glanced at the oxygen levels. "We'll need to land soon, or we'll be out of air."

She programmed in the coordinates to the nearest landing strip and, taking over manual control of the ship again, steered the thrusters southward on the planet. Now, caught in the planet's gravity, the *Scout* sailed toward the planet. I strapped into my seat in the pilot's bay.

Grabbing the radio, Mila scanned for frequencies but couldn't find any.

Into her headset, she announced, "This is the *Scout*, to all stations, requesting permission to land."

We only got static in response.

"There really should be someone responding to incoming ships," Mila frowned. "I mean, I know it's a small farming planet, but *someone* should be managing incoming radio comms ..."

Mila frowned as she spotted the green light across the clouds. "What is that? Could it be hail?"

We drew closer to the planet and could now see the continent we were aiming for below us.

As we passed through the green-tinged clouds, suddenly there was a crackling of lightning, and the sky around us turned a bright white.

"What the heck?!" I squealed.

Suddenly, all the *Scout's* systems on the nav panel turned off. The ship dropped like a stone. The air outside the ship kept crackling with lightning. The sky rippled with colour, changing rapidly across the spectrum. Bright pink. Yellow. Green.

"We've been fried!" Mila cried. "Rebooting the engine!" She slammed her fist on a button on the dashboard.

"But we've got no power!" I clawed at my seat's armrest.

"I saved some for landing-" The planet's surface raced towards us. We passed through the clouds. The wheat fields appeared as we plummeted towards them.

The *Scout's* nav dashboard flickered once, but went out.

Mila slammed her fist on the button again, growling, "Come on!"

My heart was pounding.

A farmhouse reached up towards us.

"Mila - we're going to crash!"

"Just give it a minute -"

"We don't have a minute!"

We were screaming towards the surface.

Mila smashed the button. "Come on, baby!" she yelled at the ship. The dashboard lights flicked on. The engine roared to life.

She grabbed the brake lever and jammed it to the top. I was thrown forward in the seat as the thrusters broke our freefall. But we didn't slow down enough. We were too close and going too fast for the brakes to truly soften the landing.

"Brace yourself!" Mila cried, "We're going to cr—"

***

"And the injector coil is fried," Mila called, walking out of the *Scout's* entry hatch, holding up a metal object that looked like it had been tossed in a fire.

She shaded her eyes against the bright Birumu sun. Surrounded by wheat fields, the only sliver of shade was provided by the *Scout* itself. We'd landed on the landing strip of one of the towns. The only indicator that the dirt track was a landing strip was the painted white lines on the path. We'd skidded along the strip and careened into what looked like a freshly tilled field. Soft dirt had sprayed wildly into the air, which was a rather soft, if not spectacular, landing. We'd remained strapped into the seats as we landed, so other than being shaken up, we were fine. This was undoubtedly due to Mila's rigorous safety checks each week. Even the ship itself looked okay from the outside. There was a big dent on one side, but Mila didn't look too concerned. "That has always been a little wonky. Nothing a mallet can't iron out," she'd said dismissively. The real damage was the engine, which had been fried as we'd fallen through what appeared to be an electrical storm.

Above us, the sky was a ripple of colours: reds, yellows, greens - like an aurora in the middle of the day.

When I'd first seen the sky, I'd gasped. "What the heck is that?"

"Um?" Mila frowned, not having an answer either. "I suppose that's what fried the *Scout*."

Mila had begun an inspection of the ship, logging what things could be repaired and what could be replaced. A lot of it seemed she could make a workaround or could easily swap out with a common item. Except for the injector coil that she now held. Which was charred like a potato left in the hot coals too long.

"So, what does that mean?"

"It means we're grounded. The ship is just a big paperweight. We can't leave the planet until we get a new coil."

I sighed and sat in the meagre shade the *Scout* provided. I shaded my eyes and looked down the dusty road towards town. A sign, peeling from sun and age, read *Kieta's Creek* in several languages. Mila had looked at her navcomm and frowned. There was no signal on it.

"At least we've got plenty of solar to recharge the batteries," I said. "And, you know, oxygen."

Mila grabbed a backpack from inside the *Scout* and strapped it on.

"I hope the locals are friendly. And have a mechanic."

"Let's find out."

"And Addi, we don't want to draw any attention to ourselves here. We're lying low."

"Got it."

And we started down the path to town.

The first thing I noticed about Keita's Creek was that there seemed to be no creek. In fact, the planet was so hot and dry that I wondered if the name had been in jest. As we walked into town, the old wooden buildings and main dirt road looked like a provincial town from a one-credit novel. Unlike Prema, there were no crowds, no robots, and no glowing signs.

"There aren't many chain stores here," Mila commented, looking at all the family-run storefronts, "Usually, at least a few corporations would be in a town this size."

"Maybe it's too far out?" I suggested.

And Mila pursed her lips and then murmured, more to herself, "If they can infiltrate a war-zone, I think a backwater farming planet isn't beyond them."

The locals drove solar-powered trucks and looked to be going about their business at the pace of a bygone millennium. They dressed in clothing similar to what I'd seen on Prema: long shirts and pants for working the land. We passed a grocery store, a bank, a tavern, a school, and a potter. We walked past a circular building that I suspected was a church, only because it had a lightning bolt across the front doors.

Halfway down the main street, we spotted a mechanic's garage with a hand-painted sign reading *Holgarth's Garage*. A few tractors were parked in the driveway. We stepped in, and our eyes adjusted to the cool, dark workshop. It was like a maze of engine parts and metal frames balanced on teetering piles.

There were slabs of tractors and engines scattered across every bench. One crate even looked like there was a metallic robot arm sticking out, which was odd because it seemed this planet had no robots. A computer sat on the workbench, whirring away with code on the screen with several devices connected. It looked like one of the devices had a faded logo that read *Evo*. I pointed it out to Mila, but she shrugged. If Evo made tractor parts, it would make sense that an old drive of theirs would be hacked and reused on a far-flung planet. Despite the stacks of machinery, there didn't seem to be anyone here.

"Hello?" Mila called out. She peered at the items on the shelves. "There aren't a lot of ship parts here," she reported.

There was a screech from the back of the shop. A girl. Mila and I started as the voice continued: *"Jon!* You never let me do anything!"

"I told you, Nega, I need it for *work*. I'll be finished in a few hours."

"You said that *yesterday*!"

"Yeah, but a new job came in. You can play *Princess Palace* on the weekend-"

A door at the rear of the garage slammed open. A girl who couldn't be more than ten raced to the computer in front of us, about to unplug the connected devices. Jon raced out after her, arms outstretched, ready to grab her by the collar.

"No - Nega, if you unplug that, I'll need to start again-"

And they spotted us at the same time, freezing on the spot.

Jon looked about Mila's age. He had dirty blonde hair and an oil-stained jumpsuit. He cleared his throat. "Uh. Welcome to Holgarth's Mechanics. How can I...?"

"Hi. We're looking for a new injector coil," Mila said, holding up the ship part.

He stepped over to Nega and gently peeled her fingers from the computer cables before she could disconnect anything.

"Nega, go see if Tim needs any help in the cafe," he said, giving her a gentle nudge in the direction of the exit.

"I'm telling Mum all about this," she glowered.

"And she'll say you've played too much *Princess Palace* this week already!" he called after her. He turned to us with an awkward laugh. "Sisters! Can't live with them, can't live with them." I was pretty sure that was not how the phrase was meant to go.

Mila held up the coil to draw his attention to it again.

"Sorry," he said, wiping his oily palms on his jumpsuit. "Let's start over. I'm Jon."

"I'm Mila. And this is Addison."

"You're looking for a new injector coil?" he asked. "For what? Not a tractor. A ship?"

"Yeah, a Stargrazer model."

"A Stargrazer, huh?" He turned to look at the shelves and started digging around in some of the piles of parts. "When did you ladies arrive? I haven't seen you around."

"Just yesterday," said Mila.

"Yesterday?" he frowned. "The electrosphere wasn't open yesterday."

"The what?" I asked.

"The electrosphere," he gestured above him, indicating the sky somewhere beyond the ceiling. "The electrical field around the planet? It would fry any ships that would land when it's around — *Oh.* That's why you need the new coil. You better tell your pilot to wait for the signal next time they come in."

Mila pursed her lips. "I'm the pilot."

"*Oh.*" Jon said, reddening, "Of course. Well, um, wait for the signal. The storm clears every few weeks, and you can pass through."

"Every few *weeks?*" Mila and I asked together.

He shrugged. "Yeah, that's Birumu."

Mila folded her arms. "Do you have a new coil?"

Jon shook his head. "No, but we can order one in."

"Which will be when?"

"A few weeks," he said, "Give or take."

"Okay, about payment - my navcomm isn't working-"

Jon started laughing and then, at Mila's sharp gaze, stopped abruptly.

"Sorry. Oh, you *are* new. Uh - navcomms don't work here." And, now, sheepishly, he pointed to the ceiling overhead, indicating the electrosphere again.

Mila sighed. "Okay, um, do you know anywhere that, um, pays in whatever currency you use on this planet?"

The thought for a moment and then said, "We use cash here. And as for work, I would head over to the Ag Store. There's a noticeboard there which usually has work available. Might be someone is after a farmhand."

"Okay. Thanks. You'll order the part for us?" Mila confirmed.

"Of course. Just give me a deposit in the next week or so, and I can put the order in queue to be sent offworld the next time the electrosphere opens," he said. "The Ag Store is a few blocks down on your right. And, uh, welcome to Birumu," he said, shoving his hands deep in his pockets.

"Thanks! See you around" I smiled, and he grinned back, dimples in his cheeks showing.

Now we just needed to find work.

TWO

We found the large barn on the edge of town, which had a sign reading *Agricultural Supplies*. There was only one truck parked outside. Four men in matching pale cotton shirts were loading sacks into the tray, which was full-to-teetering, with a high stack overbalanced on one side. They still had more sacks to load in but looked baffled as to how they might fit them.

"This way?" one asked.

The other, frowning, said, "No. Too big," and then stood silently, like the task of rearranging the sacks to be even across the tray was a little too challenging to comprehend.

I tried to smile hello, but none of them noticed me there.

As we headed inside, we passed even more of these silent men carrying sacks to the truck.

After the heat of the road, inside the Ag Store was blissfully cool. It was a tall and wide warehouse with rows of neat shelves packed to the ceiling. There were tractor parts, fertiliser, hay, seed, compost and even water barrels. It smelled overwhelmingly of compost and hay.

When we headed inside, I spotted the woman at the till counting real paper money. A limitation of not having nav-comms was a world that uses *paper* money. She had a no-nonsense look about her and wore a flannelette shirt rolled up to the elbows, tucked into brown pants. Her long grey hair was pinned up with what looked like diamonds. She served a man who was, despite the hot weather, wearing a formal black waistcoat. He yelled at one of the men, "If it doesn't fit, make it fit!" The pale-shirted man frowned, as if trying to understand someone speaking through water. "Put the sacks *in the truck!*"

The woman averted her gaze, looking like she was holding her tongue.

"I will *show you*." The man shook his head, glowering. He turned to the woman and spat, "I just don't know where you get good help these days."

The woman looked like she could no longer hold her tongue. "They aren't 'help', though, are they, Mr Pesce? Aren't they being reformed?"

Mr Pesce ignored her question and stormed outside, not seeming to even notice us, calling, "I'll be back once I've sorted this!"

The woman turned to us and, not recognising us, raised her eyebrows.

"Hello? How can I help you?"

"We've just arrived on the planet, and we're looking for work," Mila said.

"Just arrived?" the woman frowned. "But there's not an opening in the electrosphere for weeks."

"We are aware of that now," Mila said a little bitterly.

"*Ah*," the woman said, a hint of a smile on her lips. "Well, welcome to Birumu. I am Elin; I run this store here in Keita's Creek. I'm sure I'll be seeing you a lot - most people need a thing or two from here in their time."

"I'm Addison," I said, leaning forward to shake her hand.

Mila introduced herself. As Elin shook Mila's hand, her eyes widened at her firm grip. "Oh, you're not afraid of hard work, are you?"

"No, ma'am. We're looking for work, as we mentioned. We heard there was a noticeboard here?"

"There is..." Elin said, gesturing to a fairly empty-looking board that looked like the only notices were for lost rodents and for an upcoming dance. "But listen, I think I might be able to sort you out. Just give me a few minutes on the ham."

She headed into a back office and made a call on whatever a ham was.

I could hear the man outside yelling at the workers. Mila tucked her hands in her pockets, eyes closed, face thrust toward the ceiling like she was silently cursing the electrosphere.

Elin strode back in and announced. "I've got it sorted. Mr Larsen is looking for farmhands. Are you okay with farm work?"

"Of course," Mila nodded.

"Thank you!" I beamed.

"He's heading into town shortly anyway, so he can take you to the farm, and he will arrange for your ship to be transported there, too."

"Thank you, Elin," Mila said.

"Can I get you girls some lemonade?" Elin asked as we waited for Mr Pesce to finish yelling and the people outside.

Mr Larsen was a tall, solid man, built like an oak. He was also wearing a flannel shirt, but it wasn't ironed. He had salt-and-pepper hair. He strode in, beaming.

"I asked Hardhugadr to send me some help, and by gosh, he delivered!" he pumped Mila's hand, then mine, grinning. "Your timing couldn't be better. It's a big harvest this year, and the next electrosphere opening meant no one would arrive for weeks."

"Hardhugadr works in mysterious ways," Elin agreed.

"But he always works through you, Elin," he said with a wink, and her mouth twisted to hide a blush.

"There's food and board," Mr Larsen explained to us, "But long days. Have you worked on a farm before?"

I raised my hand. "Yes, I grew up farming," I said, but I didn't mention that it had been all by hand in a forest and not using the big tractors and machinery used by farms on planets like these.

"We can do it," Mila confirmed, and Mr Larsen beamed.

We clambered into Mr Larsen's truck and drove out to his farm. We explained about our ship hitting the electrosphere and how we needed work for a few weeks until we could repair the ship.

The dusty road toward his farm was a long, thin track surrounded by wheat, tall, golden brown and ready to harvest. We could see miles across because the land was as flat as a pancake all around us. In the distance was a low set of hills, like a sleeping dragon.

His farmhouse was a two-story building that had seen better days. It needed a coat of paint and the door hinges to be oiled. But so did the whole farm. *Larsen's Flour* was, in fact, a one-man operation, reliant on seasonal workers from off-world.

Mila was delighted that our ship had been delivered and placed to the side of the large red barn. It was the only building on the property other than the peeling farmhouse. We packed a few bags from the *Scout* and headed into the house, where we'd stay while we worked here.

We opened the creaking door and stepped in with a sigh, as the temperature was significantly cooler inside. The walls were covered in peeling paper with a floral design, and the sofa was old but had matching cushions. It was as if someone else had decorated this place a lifetime ago. That person was not Mr Larsen. The house smelled of bread, dirt, and engine oil.

On one of the walls was a photo of Mr Larsen as a young man on his wedding day. It wasn't a perfectly posed photo - it was a small group; they were distracted by something someone was saying. In the centre was a young Mr Larsen. The woman in the gold wedding dress had a cheeky glint in her eye, and Mr Larsen laughed without reserve. The bridesmaid and best man to the side were caught mid-laugh, teeth out, eyes squinting.

Mr Larsen pointed to a room at the top of the stairs, which Mila and I would share. In the bedroom, a window seat separated two old wooden beds on either side of the room. The room smelled of lavender, as though Mr Larsen had stuffed the plant into the pillows. Despite this, the musty smell of the unused room still lingered. We each had our own dressers, the room a neat little mirror image. I dumped my backpack at the foot of the bed on the left and sat. The springs squeaked unhappily.

"Cosy," I said.

"I've been in far worse places," agreed Mila. I stretched out on the bed and watched as Mila started folding her jumpsuits into the dresser.

She laid out a set of ship manuals on the bedside table, and I rolled my eyes.

"What is this? Bedtime reading?"

"Of course," Mila said.

I laughed. "Don't you ever switch off?"

"There's too much to do," she shrugged.

After a minute, I turned to Mila. "Where is his wife? Did you see that photo downstairs? Of Mr Larsen on his wedding day."

Mila pursed her lips. "Divorced people don't keep up photos of their exes all over the walls."

"So... you think she passed away?"

She shrugged and grabbed a towel from the dresser.

"But did you notice Elin in those photos? As the bridesmaid?"

I shook my head.

"She had different hair, but definitely her." Then she held up the towel and gestured in the direction of the bathroom. "I'm going to use a week of water rations in this shower."

"Enjoy," I laughed and grabbed my backpack to unpack my bag.

I shoved my dresses into the drawer and laid out my journal on the bedside table. I placed the bioluminescent mushroom from Prema on the dresser to act as a nightlight. Not that I needed it, but after what happened on Prema, I suspected Mila did.

The next day, we started work. Mr Larsen headed out to the fields on his tractor while we sorted the wheat in the barn.

"When can we drive the tractors?" Mila had asked him as we headed out for the day.

"Do you think you can handle it?"

"It'll be just like driving a spaceship," Mila had grinned.

Mr Larsen had laughed and then promised he'd show her the ropes later in the week. But for now, the wheat needed sorting. There was an electrosphere opening in a few days, and we needed as much wheat ready for sale as possible.

When I stepped inside the barn, it seemed bigger than my entire village in Nimbaii. We'd been inside that earlier that day, where Mr Larsen had shown us the whole production line with different tools to prepare the wheat.

Bundles of wheat were strung upside down on racks to dry. The place smelled earthy, like potatoes, and the din of the insects outside the barn became persistent background noise. So much so that I often needed to shout for Mila to hear me.

Up in the rafters, we could hear rodents scuttling around. Sola, the cat, clambered up the beams with death-defying agility and then settled in to stalk his prey silently. The first time that a set of the little furry rodents fell from the ceiling, we jumped, startled, until we spotted that Sola had puffed up his fur and sparks of static electricity were rippling over his fur, which he used to paw at - and zap the life from - the rodents. As a group of them huddled together, one bolt of electricity would course through them all, and they fell from their perch like a string of grapes; Sola would let out a self-satisfied little chirrup and then prance down to fetch his prey.

Mila had looked open-mouthed at the proceedings, but I'd simply shrugged. "If Sola doesn't catch them, they'll eat all the wheat."

Getting to work, I pulled one of the sheaves of wheat off the drying rack. I placed the top in a linen bag. I whacked the bag against a stone block that Mr Larsen kept in the middle of the barn. I checked inside the bag, and the wheat grains had separated from the stalks. The stone was blackened down the side because it had been struck by lightning once. It was good luck, Mr Larsen had said. After a few minutes, I checked the stalks were clean, and I pulled them out and placed them on a pile of compost. I threw the linen bag into a pile with the other bags we'd already completed. They were ready for winnowing, which we'd do later in the week.

Mila followed suit, grabbed a sheave of wheat, and started hitting the stone block enthusiastically.

"My arms hurt already," I complained after a few minutes.

"Just keep at it. Build up those guns!" Mila said, flexing her round biceps.

"It's easy for you! You're already strong, so it's easier for you."

"I started out with weak little muscles like yours, Addi. I worked at it every day to get these amazing arms." Modesty was not in Mila's vocabulary.

"That's not what I want to hear, Mila," I rolled my eyes. "I want a magic spell that can sort this wheat for us."

Mila looked at me, raising her eyebrows pointedly.

"What?"

Mila poked her head out the door to ensure Mr Larsen wasn't within earshot. "... Can't you do your plant magic thing?"

My face burned. "It's not *magic*. And it doesn't work that way. It needs to be living. And besides, I - I haven't been able to do it. Not since we left Prema."

"Not at all?"

"I've been trying to get plants on this planet to respond like they did on Prema. Nothing."

"Is it this planet? With the --" and she gestured toward the ceiling as Jon had done.

I shook my head. "It started on the ship. I tried to grow more kronox beans, and nothing happened."

"That Ancient One gave you those powers for a reason, Addi."

"Yeah, because it was asking for help. And we left it there."

"Cut yourself some slack, Addi. It wasn't that simple."

"We need to go back and rescue it. I promised."

"And we will. Once the *Scout* is repaired."

I grabbed a fresh linen bag and a new sheaf and started hitting against the lightning stone.

"So, you really can't sort this wheat for us?" Mila asked hopefully, and after my pause that stretched the distance between here and Prema, she sighed, "Oh well. It's a good workout."

We looked up at the wall of hundreds of shelves of wheat in front of us. Mila handed me the next sack.

That evening, I sat in my nightdress, watching the electrosphere against the night sky. The sky wasn't black like back on Nimbaii. It had a glow, like painted glass that moved like the ocean. There were patches of blue, pink and yellow sky against the pinpricks of stars. It was like watching a painting come to life every night.

My arms were sore from threshing wheat all day; tomorrow, it would be the same again. It was strange to build a new routine after so many weeks of the same routine on the ship. On our voyage here, in the mornings, Mila would check the ship for any overnight alerts and then exercise. I couldn't run as I used to in the forest, but I could do some aerobics, which I did while Mila did her body weight exercises.

I'd read or work on the vegetables in the growtank while Mila headed down the engineering hatch because, apparently, there were always things that needed fixing or cleaning. We'd make lunch together, occasionally adding some kronox beans into the mix, and in the afternoon, I'd watch vids about other cultures or learn how to use the navcomm and other devices around the ship. Mila would be plotting courses or checking in on our energy consumption levels.

In the evening, we'd watch entertaining vids on the small navscreen. Her favourite series was a drama that followed a princess on a distant planet who secretly trained as an assassin. The princess, of course, was in a love triangle or two and needed to kill a handful of suitors as needed to protect her secret.

Some nights, we'd play cards. Mila would insist that I learn how to memorise what was in the deck so I would know what cards were left as we played a hand. One night, on the ship's birthday, we split an entire bottle of cider she'd been brewing in engineering. She revealed that card counting in poker was illegal on quite a few planets but insisted that it was only a problem if you got caught and that it was quite a reliable source of income. The next day we went over our rationed amount of water as we nursed our headaches.

Mila entered the room in her nightclothes, ready for bed. I said, "I'll never get sick of watching this electrosphere."

"It's pretty amazing, isn't it?" she agreed, hanging her towel on a rail behind the door to dry.

"Is Mr Larsen asleep?"

"Yes. He is on the couch. Episode seven hundred and twelve of the Dodger Jones Mysteries playing through. I paused it, but I don't know how much he missed."

Mila sat next to me, watching out the window. The sky shifted to purple, then a hint of aqua.

"Do you think we'll be able to repair the *Scout*?"

Mila shrugged. "The *Scout* is an old model, so I'm not sure if the parts even deliver out here. All we can do is wait and see. But in the meantime, let's keep a low profile. No one here knows who we are, and Evo doesn't know about us being on the planet. So let's keep it that way."

"... What are we going to do?"

"About Evo hunting us?" Mila asked, sitting next to me.

"Yeah."

Mila sighed. "I felt like I knew what I was doing when I was trying to find where Bianca was. My task was simple: find where she was. Get her back. I thought I was *so close* to finding her. But now they are hunting *us* - I don't know what to do anymore."

"We will find your sister."

"I hope so."

I squeezed her hand.

"We're a team. We can do it."

Mila rolled her eyes. "And what a team we make. A pilot without a ship and a girl with the power to control plants, but only when we're in a sewer."

"Well, your ship is *almost* fixed. And I'm sure I'll get my powers back. There must be a reason I got them. And a reason they stopped working."

Mila stood up and turned out the light. "We've got a long day tomorrow."

She crawled into her bed, and I crawled into mine. The room glowed a soft blue from the bioluminescent mushroom, and green lights flickered from the muted electrosphere-coloured sky.

"Goodnight, Mila," I said.

"Night, Addi," she responded. Then, after a beat added, "I'm sorry you lost your powers."

"Me too," I said as a hollowness sunk into my chest.

THREE

I dreamed I was back home in my forest on Nimbaii, running the trails with Lian. I knew the long trails well. I dodged tree roots bulging over the path and lept over holes on the track. Lian pointed to a tall tree ahead and raced to climb it as we did when we were children.

Scrambling up the rough bark, hand over hand, we climbed so high that the ground was lost below us. But as we made our way up, I could see the tree transform into the Ancient One from the Evo spacestation. As new branches bulged out and leaves sprouted about us, the branches bulged and twisted like an eel. Lian lost his grip on the branch and fell away into the darkness, screaming, "Addi!". Against the tree bark, my hands fizzled with electricity, and then it turned into fire. The tree started burning, and it became ash.

I woke up with a start.

My night dress was drenched. The morning light streamed in through the window, making my head throb. I sat up, clutching my head. I'd had dreams like this for weeks. The guilt of not being able to help the Ancient One from the Evo spacestation was getting to me. I promised I'd rescue it, but now I was trapped on Birumu playing farmhand. I shook off the dream.

I wondered, not for the first time, why these new powers worked on Prema, but since then, they'd lain dormant. I could meditate and connect to plants like I'd always been able to do, but the ability to *control* plants–had gone. I felt a hollowness in my stomach. It had seemed for a moment like I had a purpose in the world and a way to truly control the world around me. And then it slipped from my fingers. If it was something I did or just a one-time gift from the Ancient One, I just didn't know.

My heart ached for Perse. And my parents. Even Lian. For anyone who understood what it was to be a biokin. Anyone who could help me understand what was going on.

I crawled out of bed. Mila had likely gone for a run. Her bed was made like it was vacuum sealed.

In the bathroom, I washed my face. It looked pale, and there were bags under my eyes. I pulled my cotton dress on and tugged my hair back in a loose ponytail.

In the kitchen, I grabbed some oats for breakfast, and on the front porch, I sipped a cinnamon-spiced coffee and watched the morning sun warm up the wheat fields. Sola curled up to me, his purple eyes blinking up at me. I tentatively petted him. I didn't get a zap, so he curled up on my lap and fell asleep as he absorbed the sun's rays. Later, I knew his fur would crackle with electricity.

It has been days since I last meditated, and I was feeling off-centre. Back home, we meditated daily to keep our skills honed, but I'd gotten lax here. It didn't help that on Prema, I could suddenly talk to plants, and they'd do my bidding - but after that night in the sewers, my new powers evaporated. I wasn't sure what I had - or hadn't done - for my powers to disappear.

But not meditating wasn't helping anyone. I gently nudged Sola awake, and he chirped irritably as he clambered off my lap.

Before I headed out to meditate, I knocked on Mr Larsen's office door, just by the kitchen. "Coffee is on!" I called in.

"Thanks!" he called back through the door.

On the porch, I stepped over Sola, who had immediately fallen asleep where I'd been sitting. I'd considered meditating in the vegetable patch, but I was worried Mr Larsen would spot me and start asking questions - we hadn't exactly been upfront about me being a biokin - so I walked into the nearest wheat field, just behind the farmhouse.

The stalks were taller than me, planted in neat rows. I picked a row and walked for a few paces until I was out of view of any windows. I brushed the wheat with my fingers to feel its smooth, grassy texture. The earthy smell of the field filled my nostrils, and my boots sunk into the rich soil as I took each step. The cool morning air made me shiver a little.

Having worked my way out of view, I sat right down in the soil. It was strange sitting here, hiding in the wheat field to meditate. I was a lifetime away from my village. A month ago, I would have been doing my training to become a healer with Perse and scouting for herbs at dawn. I'd have been finishing essays at school and swimming with Lian. And sitting meditating in the town square for homework.

My stomach twisted when I thought of Lian. I'd not talked to him properly before I left on my pilgrimage. And now, my heart thudded as I was coming to accept that I might not be just away for a year like I'd planned, but I was in hiding until I could rescue the Ancient One on the Evo spacestation. Which might take years. I didn't know if I would ever see Lian or my family again. I sighed. Worrying wouldn't change the past or the present, so I focused on meditating.

I gently hooked my fingers around a nearby stalk of wheat. I took a deep breath, closed my eyes, and focused on the sounds around me.

I could hear the engine fire up from the barn as Mr Larsen turned on the truck. The sound of water straining through the pipes inside the house as Mila showered after her run. Wheat whispered in the breeze, cicadas were already chirping, and birds, high above, were piercing the air with their cries. The scent of grainy wheat and earthy soil flooded my nostrils. I remembered sitting with Perse in the forest of Nimbaii, training over and over again, learning to connect with, read and seek the plants who called our forest home.

The wheat stalk settled in my hand, smooth and thin. And, in a moment, I connected to the wheat. In my mind, the wheat lit up like a firefly, and the stalk in my fingers connected to all the stalks around it, which also glowed only for my eyes. I could feel all the wheat around me reaching for the sun, greedily eating up the sun's rays. "Are you okay, little wheat?" I asked it. They didn't respond but simply reached up to the sky, with no past or future, only the now. I stretched out my connection further. One metre around me, then two, feeling the golden thread of each plant interconnected.

I then stretched my awareness out beyond the field I was in into the next field. I reached my mind out further and further, across fields and fields with - thousands of individual plants connected to me, but I hit my limit, and I couldn't stretch further. My link to the plants wavered. I was out of practice and was sure I could reach further a few weeks ago. I pulled my connection in close and focused on the one plant in front of me. I wanted to find out if I could use the powers the Ancient One gave me on the spacestation.

"Grow," I whispered, focusing my energy on it. "*Grow*."

But I didn't feel a flash of electricity. The plant didn't grow or move at my will. It remained unchanged. I dropped the connection, annoyed with myself.

Was it me? Or something else?

I sighed, standing. Huffily, I marched out of the wheat field, brushing off the dirt from my dress.

As I rounded the corner of the farmhouse, I spotted that Mr Larsen had parked the truck to the side of the house. "Are you two heading in with me today?"

"Yes!" I called. "I'll get Mila!".

Yesterday, Mr Larsen agreed to pay us in advance for a few days of work so we would order the part for the ship. He'd handed us a stack of paper bills, and Mila just frowned, not sure where to put it. I'd rolled my eyes and tucked the pile into my journal, using the leather clasp to keep it in place.

Now, I ran up the stairs, calling, "Mila! Mr Larsen is ready to take us into town!"

I opened the door, and Mila was pulling on a shirt. "S - sorry!" I stammered, trying not to blush, especially as I knew she'd just roll her eyes.

One night she'd undressed right in front of me, and I, face flushing, had looked the other way, but she laughed, "We've got the same parts!"

Mila was now pulling on her shoes, and I grabbed my backpack. "I'll see you down there!" I said, my words coming out in one breath.

We headed out a gate which was the boundary to Mr Larsen's farm. The wheat looked different as we drove along and surveyed the other fields around us. Thinner and taller. And I spotted an automated tractor the size of an entire village at work. It was harvesting the wheat, threshing it and winnowing it all at once.

"Wait - robots work on this planet?" I asked incredulously. I couldn't believe I'd been threshing by hand for weeks when a robot could be doing it!

Mr Larsen laughed. "Robots only work with some of the wheat strains. The bio-crops. I don't use that kind. I like to keep it authentic," he called back over the engine.

"Oh," I said, face flushing.

"Besides, I hear they are a nightmare to manage. They work for a few weeks, then shut down because they are waiting for the new software to be installed. And they only get downloaded when the storm clears. Ultimately, they aren't designed for a planet with an electrosphere."

"Right," I said, thinking that I'd opt for farmhands too if the only way I could collect wheat would shut down on a whim for weeks on end.

Mila tapped my shoulder and, as I turned, plucked a head of wheat from my hair. Then, with a wry smile, she pocketed it.

As we drove past one of the wider roads, Mr Larsen turned to us and called, "That's the Bees End turnoff. See those mountains?" he pointed to the small hills in the distance, "There are the most amazing waterfalls on the entire planet there. It's worth a visit when you've got a weekend."

"We'd love to!" I called back. I thought about the last waterfall I'd seen. Swimming with Sabine and Lian back home. Back before Sabine left. And before Lian proposed to me. And before I was on the run.

Mr Larsen pulled outside the Ag Store, and we headed in to say hi to Elin and to thank her for setting us up with Mr Larsen.

"Girls, it's so wonderful to see you!" Elin called as we strode in. "How are your ship repairs going?"

"Good," said Mila, even though it was slower than she'd like. "Just need to order a few parts from the mechanic, and then she should be back up and running."

"I am so impressed that you've nearly repaired it. Most ships don't ever run again after hitting the storm."

"We, er, had most systems off as we came in, so I think that saved most of the parts."

"Sounds like it certainly did!" Elin nodded. "Okay, girls - I'll let you get back to your day. You'll need to drop by for dinner.

Oh! Unless you'll be at the dance?" she pointed to the flyer on the noticeboard.

Mr Larsen started shaking his head, and Mila blanched. But I was grinning ear to ear. *"A dance?"* If I was going to learn about a new culture on my pilgrimage, a dance would be the place to do it.

"Arvold, didn't you tell them? It's going to be a great night! It's our annual midsummer dance this weekend. All the folks come from around to celebrate. Arvie will be there."

"I - I wasn't -" Mr Larsen began.

"Don't be silly. You can miss an episode of the Dodger Jones Mysteries for one night," Elin chided.

Mr Larsen's ears reddened, and Mila coughed to hide a smile.

"We'd be delighted," I grinned.

Mr Larsen and Mila looked distinctly uncomfortable, but Elin was beaming, hands touching as if about to applaud.

"Well, we'd better go," said Mila, now dragging me toward the door before I could start another unwanted conversation.

"Bye, girls!" Elin called after us.

As soon as we were out of earshot, Mila hissed, *"What part of lying low did you not understand?"*

"What's the big deal? Can't we meet the neighbours?"

"The more people that know about us, the more people who can turn us in," she said, pushing open the door to the exit. The hot air hit us like a solid wall.

"I said that we were *lying low.* Now you've agreed to attend a dance?" Mila was furious. "I say these things because I've done this many times, Addi. *Don't draw attention to us.*"

"It's just Elin. She's basically Mr Larsen's girlfriend. She's not going to turn us in."

"Don't trust *anyone,*" Mila said, her eyes boring into mine.

"Do you trust me?" I asked, folding my arms.

Mila's eyes narrowed. "Don't change the subject."

"Do you trust me?" I asked again, a knot in my stomach.

After a pause, she said, "We are in this together," she said evasively. A voice in my head reminded me that I couldn't turn her in without turning myself in. She *had* to trust me.

"Listen," I said, "If we get into trouble, knowing the lay of the land will help us. Knowing the town, knowing the people in it, is a good thing. I'm not saying we *trust* everyone we meet, but at least knowing what cards are in the deck gives us an advantage."

Mila put her hands on her hips, obviously thinking I'd cornered her by reciting her own lessons in card counting back to her. "Fine," she grumbled.

I sighed. "You're right that we need to be careful. But I think that doesn't mean we can't see a bit of the planet while we're here. Besides, this planet can't get comms from off-world. Evo has next to no chance of finding out we're here unless they send someone physically here to look for us. And they have no reason to because we're an entire sector away from where they would be looking."

Mila looked at the ground, biting her lip. "Fine," she said. "Sorry if I snapped,"

"It's okay. Mila, I'm glad you're looking out for us. There is no one I'd rather have watching my back than you."

She shifted her weight uncomfortably from one foot to the other, keeping her eye contact firmly with the ground. "Are we done?"

"Yeah. Good talk." I pulled the cash from my backpack and handed it to Mila. "Let's order this thingy for the ship."

The mechanic's garage had a low buzzing sound as we entered, as the tiny fans on the computers struggled along in the heat.

"Hello!" Mila called out, and this time Jon emerged from the back, wiping oily fingers onto an apron.

"Hi!" he grinned. "It's Addison, right? And Mila?"

"Yes! We're here to pay a deposit to order the part for our ship."

"Sure! I've got the order here. I'll process it now, and the order will send through when the electrostorm window opens."

"Thanks!" I smiled.

Jon tapped away at the computer to process the order. When he was done, he restarted the green code that ran down the screen. The code looked kind of beautiful - like heavy rain falling down through the forest canopy.

"What's this computer doing? When it's not being used for *Princess Palace*?"

Jon gave a short bark of a laugh. "I'm loading the software updates for the tractors. I have a drone sitting in space collecting them. When the storm breaks, it delivers it to me, and I copy it for the farmers in the region."

"Don't those tractors usually just automatically download updates?" Mila asked.

"On other planets, they would. But the updates take a few hours to download. The window for the electrostorm openings are usually not that long. My drone can collect the update in space and then transport a memory disk down the planet with the full update at once when the storm clears. Doing it this way means the tractors don't get half an update and then malfunction there in the field."

"That's a lot of effort for updating tractor software," I said.

He shrugged. "It's how we do things around here."

I could see why Mr Larsen didn't use a robot tractor if those were the lengths people needed to go to in order to run them.

"So, did you end up finding work?" Jon asked.

"Yes! We're working at *Larsen's Flour*."

"Oh yes, he'd need the help. He doesn't use the robo-tractors. His wheat is harvested by hand, right?"

I held up my hands which were developing blisters. "Yes. These hands, specifically."

Jon laughed again, now relaxing a little. He had an easy smile that reminded me of Lian.

"Yes, the rich folks love Mr Larsen's organic flour. Handmade, authentic wheat seeds, family-run. His wife had a good mind for marketing. I don't think his farm would have survived if she hadn't come up with..." his voice trailed off. He cleared his throat. "Um, okay, I'll place the order, but it probably will take a few weeks to arrive."

"We're here for a while," Mila said.

"Okay, great, well, I can get you on the ham at Mr Larsen's farm then?"

"Yes. Thanks!"

"So I'll see you around then," said Jon, a little awkwardly. "Perhaps at the midsummer dance?"

"Yeah," I said, smiling, "We'll be there."

"And if you need dates, my friend Tim and I -"

"We don't need dates," Mila said quickly.

"See you there!" I said as we headed out of the garage. I was grinning ear-to-ear. I couldn't wait to go to the dance. The music. The clothes. The food! *This* was why I'd left Nimbaii.

We left the garage and headed back towards the Ag store. Once again, Mr Pesce's truck was there, with the men in pale cotton shirts loading the truck.

Inside, Mr Larsen was nowhere to be found, but Mr Pesce was surrounded by a few of the other quiet men. Mr Pesce yelled at Elin, who seemed quite unconcerned by the whole experience.

We could hear Elin say to Mr Pesce, "We just don't stock a large quantity of tasia. I'll see if there's more in the back. Perhaps one of these gents could help...?" she pointed to one boy in the front, with a shaved head, a few years older than myself, "It's Taewin, right? Come out the back with me and help me look."

As Mr Pesce turned to help the men outside load the truck, he spotted us for the first time. His eyes settled on us like we were dessert. My stomach dropped.

"Ladies!" he said with a bow, "What honour do we -"

"Save it, Pesce," Elin snapped. "They're Arvold's farmhands."

His eyes flashed dismissively, "Oh. In that case, get out of the way," he said, shoving past us to his truck outside. Elin and the dazed-looking Taewin headed towards the back.

Outside, we could hear Mr Pesce yelling, and I imagined he was again red-faced with spittle.

Mila and I stood for a moment in the now-empty shop.

"I'm going to try to find Mr Larsen," I said and started wandering about the shelves. There were rows of hoses, taps, tractor parts, seeds and hay. But no Mr Larsen. Amongst all the supplies, in a back corner, stood Elin and Taewin. Taewin shoved a sizeable chunk of bread in his mouth and jammed the other pieces into his pockets. This was much more animated compared to the vague, disoriented boy I'd seen moments before.

Elin started when I rounded the corner but looked relieved when she saw it was me. The boy turned to me and put his fingers to his lips.

"Are you looking for Mr Larsen?" she called to me and, at my assent, explained, "He's in my office."

I nodded and headed back through the row to the front desk.

Mr Pesce was now back and started ringing the desk bell impatiently. "Hello?" he called, "I'm done!"

Elin and Taewin returned, and Taewin now had a vacant look about him. As requested, I kept my mouth shut. If it meant inconveniencing Mr Pesce in any way, shape, or form, I was in.

"We have no more room in the truck," Mr Pesce announced. "Can you deliver the rest of the order this week?"

"Of course, Mr Pesce. I'll just ring this up."

Mr Pesce paid and left with his troupe of silent, sluggish men behind him.

Elin sighed with relief when he'd left.

"Not my favourite customer," she said with a wan smile.

"Who was that man?" Mila asked.

"He's just one of the local farmers."

"Were those men slaves?" Mila asked.

Elin shifted uncomfortably. "... Some farmers use mini-mum-security prisoners as farmhands. You know, people who stole bread and whatnot. So it's more like... rehabilitation."

"But...?" Mila asked, reading the words hanging on Elin's lips.

"They are meant to finish their sentence, be rehabilitated, and head back off-world. But Mr Pesce's prisoners somehow just never leave."

Mila folded her arms. It didn't sound that complicated at all. It sounded disgusting.

Mr Larsen ducked his head around the corner from the back office.

"Did I hear Pesce wanted the rest of those tasia mushrooms?"

"Sure did," Elin responded. "Why?"

"Did he buy all your stock?"

Elin checked her logs, "... No, not quite. A fair bit of it, though,"

"I want to buy what's left. All of it. Put it on my account."

"What would you use it for?"

"That rudding stuff? How about fertiliser? Bird food? Maybe I'd just roll around in it and gloat that he doesn't have it?" he winked.

Elin rolled her eyes, and she put the order in the till.

"Sold," she announced brightly.

Mr Larsen headed back into the office but paused in the doorway. He called out, voice ringing with urgency, "Ladies - there's something on the radio you should listen to."

We headed into the back office. It was a neat room with a large wooden desk and a hand-carved wooden radio on the desk. There was a news broadcast on.

"- Witnesses say the explosion was the largest they've seen."

"What's going on?" I whispered.

The radio continued, "Evo staff have released a statement saying that they will investigate and ensure those responsible will be apprehended to the full reach of the law."

"It sounds like an Evo warehouse has been bombed again," Mr Larsen said.

"Evo warehouse?" I squirmed.

"Again?" Mila asked.

"Someone has been bombing the Evo warehouses over the region in the last few months," He explained gravely.

"Evo is on this planet?" Mila asked.

"Oh, yes," said Mr Larsen, "All those bio-crop farms we passed on the way into town. Those are all Evo crops. Evo practically runs this planet."

"Evo *what*?" Mila and I said at the same time.

FOUR

"Evo is *here* on this planet?" Mila asked Mr Larsen again as he switched off the radio. Elin's face was drawn.

"Oh yes, most of the farmers on the planet use their bio-crops. They have warehouses here to help them ship it off-world. All part of the fees they pay."

"But *you* don't use Evo seeds?"

Mr Larsen looked at Elin before answering softly, "No. I don't."

"What's this about a bombing? Is anyone hurt?" I asked.

"No, it's an automated warehouse. Right before the electrostorm opens, when shipping to and from the planet is open, someone has been attacking Evo supplies. It's been happening for months."

"What will happen now?" Mila asked, face drawn tight.

"They'll probably send someone to investigate."

"Like, a human physically to the planet?" Mila asked, echoing my words from earlier. As Mr Larsen nodded, my stomach sank.

"So that bombing wasn't near here, right?" I asked. "You said they happen all over the region."

"It was the warehouse for Keita's Creek. Just outside of town."

Mila's face paled.

Mila was silent on the way home, and as we sorted wheat, she kept her lips pursed, planning. I knew better than to try to draw her into a conversation when she was in this mood. The afternoon was overcast; Mila suggested we head out to the fields to begin tilling since we could work outside without the oppressive heat.

We loaded up a landbike with the tilling equipment on a trailer. I climbed into the trailer while Mila drove the four-wheeled bike to the far edge of the property.

The sky was grey overhead, with a tinge of green from the electrosphere. Back home, the green in the sky meant hail. Now, it was just one of the colours of the sky.

The paddock we headed out to was the size of a jenball field. Around us were other fields sown recently, and we needed to till the soil before planting.

I started marking out the boundaries with rope while Mila crouched over the landbike, attaching the tilling equipment.

"What are we going to do?" I called out to Mila.

"Let's start with this edge," she said, pointing to the left side of the field.

"I *meant* about someone coming to investigate the bombings."

She stood up with a slight frown. "We do what we always planned to do. We lie low."

"What if Evo thinks it was us?"

"These bombings have been happening for *months*. We've only been here a few days. They probably have people they suspect already; they just need the evidence. All we do is lie low; they come, they find the bombers, and they leave. We just keep our heads down,"

I folded my arms. I really hoped she was right. The last thing we needed was Evo looking at us and then searching their records for our names and us being right there, next to a big, bright red alert.

"Do you think we should have used fake names?"

"What?"

"Like, on this planet. Should we have used fake names?"

Mila rolled her eyes. But then, a minute later asked, "What would your name be?"

I grinned. "How about Antionette? It sounds fancy."

"It doesn't really suit you!" she called back.

"You don't think I'm fancy?" I asked, and then I looked at my dress and started brushing off some of the soil and wheat stuck to it, more to her point.

"It's not like *you're* fancy!" I said, gesturing to her oil-stained jumpsuit.

"I never picked the name 'Antionette'! Besides, when you use a fake name, you should use something easy to remember. Like, a name that is your best friend or similar to your own name. So, when you're under pressure, it's easy to remember. Like you could be Anni instead of Addi."

"Oh yeah? And you would be, what? Mia?"

"Sure," she shrugged. "Or Amelia."

Mila finished attaching the cables to the tiller and then switched on the landbike, testing the tiller worked. She then gestured to it all. "Are you ready to give it a go?" she asked.

"What?"

"You need to learn to drive a landbike before we visit those waterfalls. Climb on."

My face paled. She scooted back, so I could climb on the bike in front of her.

"There is literally nothing to hit for miles.". As I climbed on, she said in a softer voice, "It's okay. I'll be here the whole time."

I sighed. "Okay, let's get this over with."

Mila tucked up close to me. I realised how cool the air had become with her warm skin against mine. The seats were uncomfortable, hard plastic. She pointed out the accelerator, brake and steering. She had me practise using the pedals before we turned it on. And then, as ready as I was ever going to be, I switched it on, and we lurched forward.

"Just don't move the steering wheel - keep it straight," she said. I was worried I'd hit a dirt clod, and Mila would fall off and be crushed under the tiller. But she kept her hands tucked about my waist, holding firm, which meant she hadn't fallen off. As we approached the end of the row, she called above the noise, "Now we're going to do a turn. It's going to be a big, wide circle. Ready?"

"No!" I called, but, despite my fears, I turned the steering wheel anyway, and we drove in a big semi-circle to do the next row.

"Okay, now, follow that other row back in a straight line. Let's go!"

By the time I'd completed the next line, my hands were sweating.

"You want to take a break?" she asked, and I nodded, hit the brakes and turned it off.

"Good job, Addi," Mila said.

I exhaled. I'd driven it, I hadn't hit anything, and Mila hadn't ended up under the tiller. That was a success. "So next up, I'll be driving the *Scout*, right?".

"I would need to be dead first," Mila laughed, climbing off the landbike.

She grabbed two flasks of water from the landbike and threw one to me.

"So, I've been thinking," Mila said. "We've been trying to work out how to get back onto the Evo spacestation so we can find out where my sister is. And to find out how to rescue your tree. But we don't actually need to *get* to the spacestation. We just need to access their network."

"What are you suggesting?"

"I think we just hack into the nearest Evo network right here on Birumu. Every Evo warehouse must be connected to their network, right?"

"So you're saying we break into an Evo warehouse and hack into their network? What happened to lying low?"

"Mr Larsen said that the warehouses are mostly automated drones. No one will see a thing."

"Supposing that's true - how do we hack anything?"

"*We* don't. But our new friend can."

"What new friend?"

"That mechanic. Jon. I think he'd do a favour for *you* if you asked *real nice*."

It took me a second to process what she meant.

"Wait... are you saying I get close to Jon and then convince him to hack into Evo? I - I don't think that's a good idea."

Mila sighed. "It's easy. You just make friends. And then there will be a time when you happen to ask your good friend if he wants to help us by using his skills to hack into Evo."

"Isn't that kind of slimy?"

"Look - he obviously already likes you. All you're doing is getting close."

"Because I *want* something from him."

"Addi, you're overthinking it!"

"No, I'm *not*!"

"Look, friends do favours for friends, right? I just taught you to drive a landbike. Friends helping friends. This is the same thing. You just happen to know he's got a skill that might be handy in the future."

"Is that why you're friends with me? Because I've got a handy skill?"

Mila folded her arms. "We're friends because we're friends."

My eyes bored into hers.

She raised her palms, conceding. "And look, you have some cool powers. But let's not pretend this is a one-way street. You needed *my* spaceship when we first met. We have things each other needs. That's what friendship is."

"That sounds like more of a *partnership* than a *friendship*."

"This is a friendship to me," she said somberly. And then it occurred to me that maybe this was the only kind of friendship

Mila ever knew. Growing up on Naas, in the middle of a war, maybe friendships were more transactional.

"Listen," she said, changing tack. "The only way you're going to rescue your talking tree, and I'm going to find Bianca, is if we get into the Evo network to find out what they've got on us. That's our only option. We are at a dead end. We have no other way to move forward. So, what I'm asking you to do with Jon is our *only choice.*"

I sighed. I certainly couldn't think of any other ideas to rescue the Ancient One. "I wouldn't even know where to begin with Jon."

"You just do what you've got to do," she said.

My stomach knotted a little. I wondered how many times Mila had set up friendships with people just for her own means. I remembered how she'd completely ignored me when we first met until she realised I could get her onto the Evo spacestation.

Mila continued. "Look, he obviously already likes you. He invited you to the dance. Just go with him. Flirt with him a little. See what happens."

"Flirt with him?" I squeaked. This was getting way more intense by the minute.

"Yeah, just flash those gorgeous eyes and pout a little. He'll fall right over."

She thought my eyes were gorgeous? I blinked, surprised; my face started to burn. Mila laughed, "Yes - just do *that.*"

I covered my face in embarrassment.

"Let's make this easier," Mila said softly. "You just make friends. Then *I'll* ask him to hack into Evo."

My stomach flip-flopped. Mila stared into my eyes. "Addi, we're at a dead end. This is our only option to rescue your tree."

I remembered, all the way back on the spacestation, the image the Ancient One sent me: a bird's feather. A cry for help. The seeds scattering in the wind. A plea to find its children.

"Okay," I said faintly. Like it was someone else talking.

FIVE

"Today's the day!" Mr Larsen called from his office by the kitchen. His office had paper maps and rosters pinned to the walls in an order that only Mr Larsen seemed to understand. As a voice chirped through the speakers of the ham radio, Mr Larsen spun around on his office chair to scribble some wild marks on a glass map of the continent. His large frame pushed his old chair to its limit, squeaking in protest.

"From nine, we've got an hour window where the electrostorm will be clear!" I checked the time. It was just after six, and the morning was already hot.

"Only an hour?" Mila asked. "For all the ships that want to land and depart and all the cargo for the planet?"

Mr Larsen laughed. "Most of the shipping is by automated drones. And as for passenger traffic, well, this isn't really a tourist centre."

True enough, I thought.

At the kitchen table, I shovelled oats into my mouth as quickly as possible, and Mila blew on her coffee to cool it.

"We've had reports from Danton Tops - the storm cleared for them a few minutes ago," he continued, "so we'd better get started." We needed to stock as much wheat into the cargo containers as possible. When the electrostorm broke in our area, the drones would start hauling their load to dock in space. Ships would then arrive in the next few days to take the cargo to their respective destinations.

We worked late to load the crates yesterday evening, but there was still more to do "just in case we've got a longer window." In the end, we were dealing with nature: a storm opening could be longer or shorter than we'd planned for.

We headed outside, stepping over Sola in the middle of the porch again. There was a long row of metal cargo containers sitting outside the barn. We'd filled them with sacks of flour ready for sale yesterday afternoon, and there were two more containers with their side door open, ready to fill.

Mr Larsen gestured towards a metallic line embedded in the soil. It was the size of a farmhouse. "Mila, can you clear this area? The empty cargo containers will be automatically returned to this spot inside this metal line, so we can't have anything in there that might confuse the drones, so we need to move the tractors."

"Yes, sir," Mila said.

"Addison, we want to have these last two containers filled with flour. Can you please get them loaded?"

"On it," I confirmed.

Mr Larsen looked both exhausted and wired. This was the most important day of the month as anything that got off-world today would be Mr Larsen's income for the foreseeable future.

I headed into the barn and started loading up flour sacks onto a landbike, driving them to the crate and stacking them inside. I was still nervous about driving, but we needed to work quickly, and I didn't have time to second-guess myself. I watched Mr Larsen use a remote control to attach a large drone to the top, its large arms clipping onto the sides of the crate. Mr Larsen owned eight drones, and six were here, but two were still in orbit, as they didn't return last month before the storm passed. They waited in a docking bay in orbit, collecting solar from the sun, on standby, waiting for the signal that they should return to Mr Larsen to continue their deliveries.

My arms ached from loading the flour into the crates, but I didn't dare complain. After all, if this shipment didn't leave, we wouldn't get paid next month, so adrenaline had me working quickly. Mila had moved all the tractors to the other side of the yard, so she'd loaded the other landbike up with flour and joined me in filling the remaining crates. We each grabbed the corner of a flour sack and carried it together.

"We've got thirty minutes until the window opens!" Mr Larsen called out to us. When he'd finished attaching the drones, he started loading the sacks into the other crate rather haphazardly at this point.

The sky above us rippled in yellows and pinks, and it looked like lightning cracked across the sky.

"Beautiful, isn't it?" Mr Larsen said, looking up. "But it means the window is almost here. Let's lock these up," he said.

We stood back as he pulled the lever on the side of the crate and sealed the cargo on our crates.

"Let's get these landbikes out of here," he said, pointing to the metal strip on the ground, "We don't want the drone to haul my bikes out into space."

Mila and I climbed on the bikes, and as we parked them by the farmhouse, the sky lit up like the centre of the sun. Lightning rippled in the sky. And then, a moment later, the sky was a perfect blue, like on my own homeworld. I could now see a flock of birds above us. Their wings were a shiny white, which usually reflected - and were camouflaged - in the electrostorm-tinted sky.

"It's open!" Mr Larsen called, and suddenly all the drones beeped, a little light on their top switched to bright green, and they all launched into the air.

Mila and I, open-mouthed, watched the drones launch in the sky. Drones from all the surrounding farms leapt into the sky like a flock of birds. There must have been a hundred drones from the area in tidy rows, soaring into orbit. Nearby, lines of drones dropped down from orbit, with individual drones peeling off to find their home base all across the region, like fireworks. Mila tapped my shoulder and pointed in the distance to a small passenger ship landing. The only tourist arriving, I thought.

Two drones settled behind the barn, dropping off their empty crates and then moving on to the full crates we'd just loaded and launched themselves and their new bounty into the sky.

The drones repeated this dance, delivering crates and picking up the new ones before Mr Larsen pointed to the green twinge in the sky in the distance. Six of the crates had been delivered, and two drones were attaching themselves to the two additional crates we'd loaded, and they sprung into the air.

"I don't think these crates will make it," Mr Larsen said, watching the pink and yellow-tinged sky creep towards us. He was watching the device in his hand, looking at the status of each drone. Six of the drones had returned and landed in the field, registering that there was no new cargo. Two drones were racing into the sky.

"Come on, you can do it!" he whispered.

But there was a crackle of lightning across the sky, and one of the crates was hit. The drone looked as if it had frozen momentarily in the air before it started to drop like a stone.

Mila and I watched it, miles above us, start to plummet to-wards us. It was falling faster and faster. I looked at Mr Larsen, who was looking to predict where it might land, lips pursed. Should we run? That would surely crush us in one go if it fell on top of us. It *looked* like it was coming straight for us. I grabbed Mila's hand, eyes wide, unsure if we should run or stay. She stood, feet firmly planted, watching the drone. I didn't know if running would put me into its path instead.

All of a sudden, a red parachute burst from the top of the drone; its descent had been broken, just for a moment. And then the little drone motor fired up again, and it hovered, recal-ibrating. The electrostorm passed overhead us, and the sky re-turned to its rainbow-tinted colour and the drone, along with its cargo, returned to the field. I unpeeled my fingers from Mila's.

Mr Larsen let out a long sigh, then turned to us with a weary smile.

"Seven containers made it to space. And while this baby didn't get there, she also didn't get fried in the storm. I'd say it's our lucky day. Thank you for all your work, ladies. I'd say we've all earned the afternoon off."

"What do you mean you 'weren't scared'?" I asked Mila as Mr Larsen drove us into town.

"I knew the parachute would go off," Mila said, "Didn't you?"

"Of course not! I *didn't know* about the parachute! How did *you* know?"

"I've been reading the manuals before bed," she shrugged.

"What kind of person reads *drone manuals* before bed?!"

"I do. I like seeing how things are built. To see if there's a feature that I can incorporate into the *Scout*."

"Yeah, I guess."

We were heading into the cafe in Keita's Creek for a celebratory lunch. Mr Larsen was in a bright mood, having shipped more crates than he'd planned. He'd said that having a drone struck by lightning and surviving was a good omen.

We were walking through town after having parked at the Ag Store. As we wandered through town, people were running errands, stopping in the street to catch up with friends. I loved being immersed in another world where so many things were the same but had lots of little differences. Everyone at night slept and dreamed and loved - but they wore different clothes and believed in different Gods. The differences about things that really mattered seemed quite small in the end.

We passed the potter again, who sold everything from dinner plates to vases and fine jewellery made of clay and stone and a few more restaurants.

"Those places are a bit too fancy for the likes of me," Mr Larsen laughed, holding out his coffee-stained shirt.

There was a school where a handful of young children were playing outside. Some boys were playing jenball, and others were playing a blindfold game. It stung me for a moment, the memory of the game I'd played as a child, which the Ancient One had played back to me as it called for help. *A stone. A feather.*

A couple of older students were crouched in a stairwell, reading textbooks and hurriedly finishing homework, and I could swear that in the far corner of the schoolyard, some older kids were jumping over the fence to skip their next class. I wondered where they were headed. Whenever I skipped school, Lian, Sabine and I would head down to the river, trying to find a cave we'd heard about but never could find. Lian was convinced that Sabine had found it one day but never let us in on it before she left.

I tugged at the bracelet that Lian gave me. I hoped he was okay. He'd be preparing for his own pilgrimage soon.

We arrived at the cafe, and it turned out to be opposite the mechanic's garage. My shoulders tightened at the thought that we'd run into Jon. I wasn't sure I was ready to "get to know him." Whatever that meant.

The cafe was wooden with a large balcony, crowded with tables. Inside, it had green lamps and a large, brightly lit display cabinet of cakes. The aroma of coffee, vanilla and chicken wafted from the kitchen.

"Hello! Are you after lunch?" The waiter was a boy around my age, and his name tag read 'Timothy'. He had dark skin and deep brown eyes and wore a chef's apron. This must have been the boy that Jon had tried to set Mila and me up on a double date with. I flushed a little at the thought.

"Hi, Tim," Mr Larsen said with the ease of someone he'd known his whole life. "We're having lunch. Table for three, please."

From behind us, a voice said, "Make that four," and we turned to spot Elin walking in.

Mr Larsen's ears reddened. "Oh, Elin! What are you doing here?"

"Same as you, I imagine. Recovering from the shipping this morning. What chaos!" Elin said, but I couldn't imagine anything in Elin's life being chaos. She was more organised than Mila.

"Four it is," said Tim, leading us to a table in the back.

As we sat, Elin recounted her morning - she had a shipment of fifteen crates come in and a large, fragile crate direct from Evo, which required four drones alone. "I couldn't imagine what would happen if the window closed and the crate just *dropped* from the sky. Even worse, the delivery was for Mr Pesce, who kept radioing every fifteen minutes to see if it had arrived."

"I hate that you have to deal with him," Mr Larsen grumbled.

"I have to do business with *everyone* on this planet, Arvie. You know that. And I'm a big girl - I can look after myself."

Elin passed the menus around to us all.

"Was that a passenger ship that landed?" I asked. "Are there new arrivals in town?"

"None that we want," Elin sighed.

"What do you mean?"

"They landed at the Evo warehouse. It means they've sent someone to investigate the bombings. *Again*."

"It better not be that repulsive-"

"Just keep your cool,"

"You *know* what he said about me,"

"I know. And he's wrong. We all know it."

"I can barely show my face in town!"

"Barely show your face! When did you ever leave the farm to begin with?" she teased.

Mr Larsen couldn't help smiling at that. "What? I visit you all the time,"

"To buy *fertiliser*."

"And it's the best part of my week," he said, winking.

Tim delivered our food - I had ordered a chilled tomato soup - and Mr Larsen told us about the waterfalls in the mountains. He shared which spots were for tourists and which spots only the locals knew. "The really beautiful ones aren't in the guide-books," he grinned, "but you need to climb a little off the trail."

I couldn't wait.

A young girl came to clear our plates - I realised it was Nega, Jon's sister - who looked bored until she spotted us.

"Oh, I remember you!" she exclaimed, "You're going to the dance with Jon!" I was? I remembered that we were going, and he was going - but the part where we were going *together* wasn't really how I remembered events happening. "Jon said he was going to ask you. Did he ask you?"

"Actually—" I started, but Mila kicked me under the table. "I mean - yes. He did. I am going to the dance with him."

Mr Larsen and Elin exchanged a look of surprise as I rubbed my now-throbbing ankle.

"What are you wearing?" Nega chirped.

"It's a surprise," I said with a tight smile.

"I can't wait to see!" Nega said, prancing away with our plates, excited, no doubt, to taunt her brother somehow.

I looked at Mila, palms sweating. What *was* I going to wear?

"Well," Elin said, pursing her lips with an expression I couldn't read, "Did you pack clothing for a dance?" Back home, I probably would have worn the dress I was wearing *now* to a dance. I shook my head, realising that this dress would not be suitable here.

"Come back to my place," Elin offered, "I've got plenty of spare outfits. I wasn't always this crone you see here. I have a lot of clothes lying around."

As we rose to leave, Mr Larsen and Elin argued over the bill - the diamonds in Elin's hair sparkled against Mr Larsen's reddening ears. Tim split the bill for them down the middle.

As I opened the cafe door and stepped outside, I almost fell over Jon, who was hurrying into the diner. As our eyes met, I flushed. I wasn't ready to do whatever I was meant to do.

"Addison!" Jon said, "I was coming to...". And he cleared his throat to start again. "Nega said she saw you and said we were going to the dance. I - I don't want you to think I had presumed-"

"It's okay," I said, "I would like to go with you."

Jon's eyebrows jumped in surprise. "You - you would?"

I nodded, "Yes. I haven't been to a dance in a long time. Maybe you can show me how it's done on Birumu."

He smiled, "Oh! Great! I would like that too! But I am sorry about Nega - she's always poking her nose into other people's business."

"It's fine," I said, reassuring him. "And it would be nice to get to know you more."

"You too," he said. And then, with a stilted goodbye, he headed into the cafe.

Tim was leaning against the doorway with a stupid grin plastered on his face. "Don't let the boss see you flirting on company time," he teased Jon.

Jon playfully shoved him on the shoulder, "It's my lunch break. Aren't *you* meant to take my order?"

"No way, man. You always order the same thing. I put the order through when I saw you leave the garage. I am lightning fast," he said, pulling some jenball moves in front. Jon laughed and dodged, then squeezed his way past Tim into the cafe.

Mila, Elin and Mr Larsen caught up with me outside. A tall blonde man with a tightly clipped beard approached from across the road. Even in this heat, he wore a suit that had an embroidered logo on this jacket that read 'Evo'.

My mouth was dry. Elin said an Evo representative had landed to investigate the bombings. And here he was. I shot a glance at Mila, whose shoulders tightened visibly.

"Look who we have here," the man drawled.

"Mr Farrell," Mr Larsen said, eyes narrowing.

"I'm back. And this time, I'll get proof of who is bombing these warehouses," Mr Farrell said, eyes drilling into Mr Larsen's.

Elin snapped, "He has nothing to do with this!"

"*Really*? I can't think of *anyone else* on this planet who has as much of a grudge against Evo as he does. He's one of the few farmers who doesn't use our crops. And, of course, taking into account his past..." he let it hang.

Mila and I exchanged a look.

Mr Larsen said, "Farrell, I don't deny that I would *love* to see Evo burn. But this has *nothing* to do with me."

Mr Farrell's eyes narrowed. "As I said, I *will* get proof this visit. Your days of freedom are numbered," and he turned and strode over to the mechanic's garage.

My hands were shaking.

"How can he accuse me?!" Mr Larson was pacing on the spot, face aflame. "He's just grasping at straws. I didn't have anything to do with it!"

"I know you didn't, Arvie. Listen, you'll be fine. You didn't do it; there's no proof, so you don't need to worry."

Mr Larsen sighed.

Elin turned to Mila and me, "Let's head back to my place to find some outfits for the dance."

Mr Larsen had some other errands to run in town - I was sure he just wanted to walk off Mr Farrell's accusations.

As we walked down the road to Elin's house, Mila slid up beside Elin.

"So, why does Mr Farrell think Mr Larsen has something to do with the bombings?"

Elin hesitated, "Look, I'm not sure it's my place to say. Let's just say that he has been on Evo's radar for a while now."

"Oh," Mila said, and she sent me a look of wide eyes that said, *so much for lying low.*

I shrugged; there was nothing we could do now and see how things played out. Mr Larsen seemed genuinely surprised when he heard about the bombing. I didn't think he had anything to do with it. Besides, he wasn't the only person on this planet who wanted to see Evo go down; I was sure of it.

In a moment, we approached a building that was nothing short of a mansion. Elin walked right in.

"We're here," she announced, and we strode into the multi-story house. We pulled off our boots and headed to the sitting room. The room overlooked a small but beautiful decorative garden through large glass doors the size of the whole wall.

"I might not have a big farm like Arvie, but I do like to get my hands dirty sometimes," she smiled, nodding to the long ferns and white flowers near a small ornamental pond. Birds flitted about it, splashing water down their backs.

"Your home is beautiful," Mila said. It was an understatement. This had to be the nicest house on the planet.

"Thank you, Mila. That's kind. It's a family home - it's been handed down for many years, and now it's mine,"

We made our way upstairs and found our way into a closet the size of my entire room back in Nimbaii. It was stuffed with dresses and outfits bulging out. "As I said, this house - and everything in it - has been in my family for generations, so there's a lot here. Some of these outfits are rather out of fashion now, but these things always circle back, don't they? Do look through to find something you like."

"Can we pick anything?" I asked, unsure.

"Of course. Obviously, don't pick the dress that *I* am wearing to the dance, but everything else is fine for you to borrow,"

I started working my way through the dresses, touching the soft fabrics, the jewels embedded in them, and the scent of rose throughout.

"What does one usually wear to a barn dance on Birumu, Elin?" I asked, skimming the silks. I wasn't sure which of these dresses would fit me.

"It's customary to choose an outfit inspired by Hardhugadr. So, yellows or white, or gold. Or with a lightning motif."

I waded through the dresses - reds, greens, black, white and my eyes settled on a midnight blue dress with lightning bolts and stars embroidered all across it. "Something like this?"

Elin laughed when she noticed the dress I'd chosen. "Oh, yes. My sister had that embroidered for a dance when she was your age. Try it on,"

I headed to the bedroom and, behind a modesty screen, started undressing, pulling off my cotton dress that was so coarse compared to this delectable fabric. It must have been made of spider silk.

I could hear Elin turn to Mila. "So, what about you, Mila? Do you like any of the dresses here?"

Mila was silent for a long time. "Er, they are beautiful...."

"I've noticed that you've never worn a dress any of the times I've met you. On your planet, is it customary for women to wear trousers?"

Mila paused a beat and then responded, "Yes?"

"Come," Elin said, tugging at some of the racks deep in the closet, "I have *just* the outfit for you."

I tugged on the blue dress and pulled together the laces. When I looked at myself in the mirror, I almost didn't recognise myself. I looked like a lady. Like someone named Antionette. The dress pulled in my waist and showed off my collarbones with a wide neck. The lightning bolts down the front were lined in a way to make me look like I actually had hips. The long skirt floated about me as I spun. I was, for a moment, a bird.

Mila stepped into the room, having pulled on her outfit right there in the wardrobe. She wore a white button-up shirt with a yellow waistcoat tucked in tight about her hips. The curve of her breasts peeked through the folds at the collar of the blouse. Her trousers were dark blue, almost black, and I could see some lightning bolts embroidered on the pockets. She approached the mirror, pulled her long curly hair on top of her head, and experimented with the look. Confidence rippled off her. Like any fool that would challenge her to a duel would surely lose.

She turned as if to me to ask what I thought, but then her eyes flickered over my dress, and instead, she sucked in a short breath.

We each stood in silence for a moment.

"You will certainly get Jon's attention in that," Mila said softly.

I swallowed hard, face burning.

Elin strode over, "Okay, ladies, turn around so I can see you!"

And she assessed us both and then clasped her hands, "Oh, no one will be able to take their eyes off you two!"

Exactly the opposite of lying low, I thought.

SIX

After the window off-world opened yesterday, Mr Larsen spent a lot of time in his office, trawling through all the comms which had arrived from off-world. The messages were downloaded directly to the computer, and he had about two months of messages to wade through. It was everything from invoices from the ships that took the wheat to their respective planets to payment notifications from wholesalers who sold it on.

And he had a whole suite of messages from people across the solar system looking to order his wheat on their planet. He had a map of the system on one of the walls, where he updated listings of how many orders from that planet.

"I need to work out how to deliver my crops to Prander," he mused to himself when I'd come with his coffee. "I could have a shipment get to Nixxilion, and then another ship travel through the Gentroy system..."

"Expanding your territory?" I laughed.

"It's not just that," he said solemnly, "It's important to get my wheat to them."

"What do you mean?" I asked, setting the coffee on the desk.

"Some of the popular Evo wheat strains have been spliced with shellfish genes to withstand the harder landscapes."

"But your wheat is designed to be hardy, too. What's the difference?"

"Each season, I select the crop which has grown best and use the seeds from that crop for next year's harvest. Doing that for a decade, I end up with a hardy crop. It's crop *selection,* not altering what wheat is."

"You mean with the shellfish genes?"

"Yes, because there's a percentage of the population allergic to shellfish who aren't aware that the bread they eat is making them sick over time."

I did the math. If Evo sells wheat to a billion people, even if one percent is allergic, that is still *millions* of people who could get sick.

"Do Evo know?" I asked.

Somehow, at that moment, deep bags developed under Mr Larsen's eyes. He said quietly, "They do. In fact, in a strange coincidence -" he said this like it was anything but - "Evo spun off the business arm that managed the wheat strain with the shellfish into a separate sub-company and then declared it bankrupt. So, the lawsuits were dissolved."

It was all at once very hot in here. "So, Evo just... wrote up some fancy documents to hide the fact that they are killing people?"

He looked at the floor. "Like I said, I'm sure it's just a coincidence."

I sat down on the chair next to him, looking at the system he was mapping across the glass wall: all the planets where he was trying to ship his wheat.

"So, it's more like a community service to get your wheat to that sector?"

He nodded, eyes settling on the image of his deceased wife. "Yes, that's it. A community service."

And now I thought I understood why Mr Farrell thought that Mr Larsen was behind the bombings. Because he sure had the motivation to hate Evo.

"You ready to hit these waterfalls?" Mila asked. With a mouth full of water, I nodded. Most places would call the landforms ahead of us hills rather than mountains, but it seemed all that the planet had, so they just picked the grandest name they could. I shook my arms and legs to stretch one last time before climbing back on the landbike.

As we travelled up the mountain road, the sprawling wheat fields were replaced by smaller vegetable farms by the roadside and, finally, forest. There were a few trucks on the roads up this path, so we could leisurely make our way up. The temperature dropped slightly as we circled higher. We passed fruit stalls and outdoor cafes serving icy treats for passersby.

We followed the route that Mr Larsen had told us about to one of the main lookouts. As we got closer, we spotted the hand-painted signs directing tourists to the viewing area.

We drove into a parking lot and parked our bikes in a spot that would have sun most of the day to recharge our bikes, and we pulled on our backpacks. We headed to the wooden lookout with a panorama overlooking a tall, thin waterfall, which fell into a river far below us. As we were in the middle of summer, the river wasn't at its height, so water dripped lazily over the edge. From this distance, we could mostly just hear the buzz of crickets from the forest and trucks on the road rather than the roar of the waterfall. The forest was tightly packed around the waterfall at its base. The earthy scent of dirt and rocks, and water reminded me of home.

"This is nice," I said, leaning over the railing.

"It is," she said, taking in the view. "But not as nice as the secret spot that tourists don't know about," and pulled out the map that Mr Larsen had drawn us. I took in the scenery for a moment longer while she inspected the map.

We headed to the far edge of the parking lot behind a short tree with thick, red leaves. She ducked behind it, and there we spotted a thin trail worn by years of teenagers sneaking to the bottom of the waterfall. Mila turned to me with a wide grin. "Let's go!"

We walked along the tight path as it followed the cliff side down. I'd climbed down rocky outcrops many times, but my heart still raced if I spent too long looking over the edge rather than focusing on the path in front of me. We worked our way down the steep hillside, clambering over boulders and gaps we needed to leap over. Small shrubs growing from the rocks created handholds to guide us across. "Thank you," I said to the shrubs as I tugged at them for balance.

As we got towards the forest at the bottom of the cliff, we could hear the river running nearby. Birds called about us. I felt a sense of calm that I hadn't experienced in a long time.

We put our feet on solid ground and followed the faded trail through the forest. Once or twice, we thought we'd lost the track but managed to find it again as one of us stayed on the path, and the other hunted about for the rest of the trail. As we picked our way through the trees, the din of the water falling from high above us grew louder.

And then, all at once, the trees opened up, and we found ourselves at the base of the waterfall, in front of a deep, clear pool. Above us, the cliff looked endless, with water gushing down from far above. Rocks jutted out through the cliff side all the way down the waterfall, and the spray from the water hitting these rocks created a scattering of rainbows. I tried to spot the lookout we'd seen earlier, but the forest in the way meant that this pool was completely secluded.

The pool was deep and clear, with large flat boulders scattered in the water, perfect for jumping off or basking on.

The air was still burning hot, so I immediately dropped my bag by the side of the path and pulled off my shoes. I slung my legs into the water.

"It's really cold!" I called out to Mila over the sound of the waterfall. But she was behind me, already pulling off her jumpsuit. Only in her undergarments, she ran to the edge of one of the rocks and dove in.

She burst from the water with a squeal, "It's freezing!" she called back.

After Mila dove underwater, I pulled off my dress and hung it on a nearby tree branch, and I, too, dove in wearing my undergarments. The water took my breath from me. Mila called, "Just keep swimming. You'll warm up!" as if I hadn't been swimming in cold water before I could walk.

We swam over to the bottom of the waterfall and climbed onto the rocks. The spray was like gentle needles in my skin. The water from high above ran over my skin and drilled into my back like a massage. I closed my eyes and let the waterfall run over me, letting it work out the tension in my shoulders and the stress of the past few weeks.

This weekend escape couldn't have come at a better time. The arrival of Mr Farrell made everyone in the farmhouse tense. Mr Larsen was tetchy and jumpy, and Mila had been very finicky about me putting things away and kept asking me when I was going to see Jon next. The answer hadn't changed: the dance.

I turned to Mila, who, eyes closed, let the waterfall massage her back. Her curls grew long and wavy under the water, draping about her shoulders, and droplets clung to her hair like diamonds. I noticed her underwear, like mine, had become slightly transparent.

I dove back into the water and found a large rock in the centre of the waterfall to sun myself on. I crawled up and spread out like a cat. Mila clambered up after me.

I closed my eyes, listening to the waterfall, the birds, and the water lapping about us. The heat of the rock below me warmed my skin while the sun toasted my back.

I rolled onto my side, toward Mila, to doze. The water sparkled over her back and legs. Her head was tucked into the crook of her arm as she lay dozing.

"We have this story back home," I said. "About where waterfalls come from."

"Mm?" she murmured, eyes closed.

"A long time ago, before space travel, the biokin lived in the forest with the Ancient Ones. Their village was under the branches of one such tree. One year, there was rain for weeks and weeks. It got so bad that it started flooding the town. The village did their best to keep the floodwaters at bay, but after all the rain, the village was about to be swept away. So they begged the tree to save them. They promised to bury offerings in its soil every year. The Ancient One agreed. It started growing right there. Its canopy grew wider, and it sheltered the whole village from the rain. It grew thick roots that surrounded the village to block out the floodwaters. It started absorbing the flood water and grew fatter and fatter. Two, then three times its size. It was so large that the village was safely nestled inside the tree, and the flood waters were still raging outside the tall roots of the tree. The Ancient Ones saved the village. Finally, when the rain ended, the Ancient One was still full of water, bulging. On the side of the tree far from their village, the biokin buried food, like they promised, but the tree couldn't absorb anything else. So it split right down the middle, and all the water gushed out and became a waterfall."

Mila smiled sleepily. "That's a nice story," she said.

"We have all kinds of stories about the Ancient Ones like that," I said, closing my eyes again. "About the way the world was created. What about you? Do you have Ancient Ones on Naas?"

She shook her head softly. "No, not like that. I don't think we had Gods." Then, after a moment, she said, "When I was little, my Mum used to tell us that the universe would know if we had behaved badly and that bad things would come back fourfold. So we needed to be good."

"Did it work?"

"My sister sure believed it,"

"You didn't?"

"I didn't really listen," Mila said. "Maybe it was true."

"That bad things came back fourfold?"

Mila was silent for a while. "I don't know. I think about the war on Naas, and losing my parents, losing Bianca and losing-" she held her sentence in the air. "Sometimes I think that the universe is coming back fourfold because of what I've done. But I don't think I caused a war, so it couldn't have been all due to *my* mistakes. I think the universe just serves what it serves."

"But some good things have happened," I ventured, "You built the *Scout*."

"That's true. And I met you," she said.

My heart started to pound.

"And I haven't been murdered in my sleep in the last few years, despite a lot of close calls," she continued.

"Oh yes, like when?" I asked.

She smiled, "Oh, like *every job* I've ever taken. For a long time, I took jobs transporting goods across the system for really nasty people. But I didn't have many options to make money when I first left Naas. All I had was a ship. I once transported a goat. A real, live *goat*. When I have the *Scout* on a high burn, the engine room *still* smells like a wet goat. And the amount of times I escaped with my life from a game of poker is beyond measure."

"Sounds like the universe is on your side, at least some of the time," I said.

"I hope so," she said. "I might have made some mistakes in my past, but I'm trying to set it right now. Hopefully, the universe sees that."

"I think so," I said, "If not, I'll ask the Ancient One on Evo to throw in a favour."

"Thanks, Addi," she laughed.

I rolled over onto my back, covering my face with my arm to block the glare of the sun.

"When I used to do this with Lian and Sabine, we used to play Mac-Moe with the rocks by the river. I would *always* win. I even started carrying my winning pebbles around in my pockets, and my mother would always yell at me to stop bringing so many pebbles home as she kept finding them all about the house."

"Lian was the guy that proposed to you?"

"Yeah," I said, my stomach twisting.

"And you said no?"

My face was hot. "He asked all of a sudden." I said defensively, "And I don't think I see him that way."

"What type do you like?" she asked, one eye watching me.

And my heart pounded faster.

"I don't know yet. I've never dated anyone. It's why I'm so nervous about all this stuff with Jon. I've never dated anyone normally, let alone pretend."

"It's easy. You just be you. Learn what he likes. Talk about things you like. You'll be fine."

"Have you ever dated someone?" I asked, voice rising awkwardly.

She was silent for a long time. "Yes. No. It was... complicated," she said. "I... we... On Nass, things are different. It was a war. The rules aren't the same as here."

"O... kay. But did you go on a date?"

"Um...." she said, frowning. "Maybe?"

"Well, what makes you think you were dating?"

She looked at me with a long stare and then answered evasively, "We did things together that people who are dating do."

"Like kiss?"

"Are you serious?" she laughed, and I took that as a yes. Or *more* than a yes. I hadn't kissed anyone before. Although, I almost had, once. At a bonfire night, back on Tevinter, Sabine had leaned in close, breath tangy with wine, and had almost kissed me. But then, some kids were herding a chicken too close to the fire, and she shooed the kids off. But the moment had passed. Soon after, she'd left for pilgrimage, and we never spoke of it again. We never even brought it up after she returned from her pilgrimage and asked me to help her leave. Because she'd fallen in love offworld. My heart dropped, pining for that life–that kiss–I would never have.

I turned to Mila, shaking off the memory. "Were you in love?"

She paused again, this time with a sigh in the air. "How do you tell?"

"I don't know," I said. "Don't the stories say that you want to be with them all the time? And they make you happy?"

She smiled a half-smile, "You could be describing a dog,"

"Well, were you dating a dog?"

She rolled her eyes and flicked some water at me. "No, I was not *dating a dog*. It was just someone. Who I'll never see again."

"Do you miss them?"

She shrugged, "Some people aren't in your life forever."

"I suppose so," I said.

Mila rolled onto her side, facing me, "So what's this game? Mac-Moe?" she asked.

I grinned, "Well, we need a set of six pebbles each," I peered off the side of the rock into the water below. "I think some good flat ones are on the bottom here."

It was getting to be late afternoon, and we finally motivated ourselves to climb back up the cliff. Along the road on the way back, we spotted one of the outdoor cafes. It was a wooden stall, and the tables were surrounded by bright yellow sun umbrellas.

My stomach grumbled. We had packed lunch - bread rolls, cheese and salad - but climbing the cliff left my stomach growling.

"Can we stop?" I called out to Mila.

"Sure!" she called.

We parked the bikes and walked to the cafe. We ordered fresh juice. The pebbles in my dress pockets clicked together as we found a table in the sun.

Mila shook her head, laughing. "I can't believe you kept those pebbles!"

"Those are the rules," I insisted. "Winner keeps the pebbles,"

As we sat at the table, Mila asked, "So, is that what you did your entire childhood? Playing Mac-Moe?"

"Not the *entire* time," I said. "There was a period where I seriously wanted to be a magician."

She raised an eyebrow. "Oh yeah? Like, what, conjure a rabbit out of a hat?"

"No," I said, "But I can pull a pebble from your ear," and using a sleight-of-hand trick I'd learned as a child, I brushed Mila's ear and presented her with a pebble.

Mila laughed in delight, "That is so *stupid*,"

"That was *magic*," I said, and I tossed her the pebble, grinning. "You know I have powers,"

The waitstaff brought our juice, and we surveyed the sunny road. Forest was packed tightly on either side of the road, and nearby birds snapped up crumbs left from previous diners. Trucks groaned by, and people pulled into the parking area for snacks. Mila held her hand up to her eyes to block the sun and pointed to someone behind me, "Hey, is that Jon?"

"Oh, very funny," I said, rolling my eyes.

"No, I'm being serious," and I turned and saw that Jon had walked up to the counter and ordered something too. He turned and spotted us and turned bright red before he regained his composure.

"Hi," he said, coming over to us, "Addi. Mila. What are you doing here?"

"We came to look at the waterfalls. You know, classic tourist adventures,"

"Of course," he said, "Yes, the falls are best in spring, but still good this time of year."

"What about you?" I asked.

He held up one of the devices we'd seen connected to his computer back in the mechanics. "I need to deliver the datadrive to a customer," he explained. "But since it's the weekend, I thought I'd take it slow and enjoy the scenery. I might go and visit the Blue Vista lookout while I'm here, too." Before I could respond, the waiter called out Jon's order, and he headed over to the kiosk.

He walked back over to the counter again, and Mila leaned over to me and hissed, "This is the perfect opportunity to *get to know him.*"

"*What*?"

"Go with him to the lookout. I'll wait here. I can entertain myself."

My clothing was damp from the swim and covered in dirt and grime. I did not feel like going on a date right now.

But before I could come up with an argument, Jon was back.

Mila said to Jon, "Addi was just saying she'd love to see the lookout. I've just ordered food, so I can't come, but Addi can."

"Oh, really? It's not far from here," Jon smiled.

I struggled to find any words. I shot daggers at Mila, who looked at me, eyes drilling into mine. And I remembered that Jon was our way to get into Evo. He could hack into their network, and we could maybe learn more about the Ancient One, and we'd be able to discover where Bianca was, and we might even learn why they had an alert on us. Any *one* of those things would be good to find out.

"Sounds great," I said, like a parrot. I made myself look at Jon and smile. He looked at me with slightly red cheeks, and I felt ashamed for not blushing like him. He did seem like a nice enough guy. Mila did say that all I'm doing is making friends. This was a good introduction.

"Do you have a landbike?" he asked me, and I pointed mine out.

"I'll just stay here," Mila said loudly. "And eat my meal. In fact, I might just go to the counter and check on it," she said, standing abruptly and giving me a shove towards Jon. "Have fun!"

Jon led the way on his landbike, and I followed. I was still new to driving and was nervous that I'd crash into something and embarrass myself. Or worse, lose any chance of getting close to Jon.

It was true that the lookout was only a few minutes away. It was a platform that overlooked the waterfall, but from this direction, we could also see the mountain descending, the winding river and the fields beyond. It was getting towards dusk, so the sun played tricks with the electrosphere, bringing streaks of yellows, greens and pinks to the sky.

We found a nearby boulder and sat down together in awkward silence for a moment.

"So, what did you get up to today?" he ventured.

I pointed down to the bottom of the waterfall, "We went swimming down there."

"Oh," he laughed, "You're almost a local now! Usually, it takes people a few months to find out about that secret location!"

"Have you been there?"

"So many times! There was one summer when Nega wanted to go *every* weekend. I think I could walk down that cliff with my eyes closed by the end of it,"

"It's a really beautiful spot." I agreed. Then I asked the only thing I knew about him, "Do you spend a lot of time with Nega?"

"It's my job as a big brother. I kind of have to watch out for my sisters."

"*Sisters*? How many do you have?"

He laughed, "I have three. But they all aren't as much of a handful as Nega. My other sisters, Becca and Kem, are a lot quieter, but they are also younger. Nega is the oldest sister, so she thinks she can boss everyone around."

"She does know what she wants," I said, laughing. "I thought I saw her working at the cafe in town?" I asked.

"Oh, kind of. Not really. I can't work if she's at the garage if she's trying to use my computer for *Princess Palace* every second of the day. So Tim lets her wait tables. It helps him out - sort of - and it keeps her out of my hair."

"It takes a village to raise a child, doesn't it?" I said. It sometimes seemed like I spent more time with Perse than with my own parents.

"What planet are you from?" he asked me.

"Tevinter," I said. "It's not in this system."

"Is it like this?"

"Oh, no. Well, it's not like *that*," I said, pointing to the farm-land, "but more like *this*," gesturing to the forest. "I lived in a forest most of my life,"

"A *forest*? I'd love to visit sometime," he said longingly.

"Yes, come and visit!" I said, figuring out I'd deal with how to let an outsider inside our forest reserve later. "Do you travel much offworld?"

He shook his head. "I've never been able to afford it. I got a job as soon as I was old enough to help Mum out with the bills - it's a house of five, after all. And Kem is actually pretty sick, so I kind of *have* to work to afford everything."

"I'm sorry to hear that."

He shrugged. "Everyone has their own stuff going on."

"... So you became a mechanic?"

"When I was in my last year of school, the mechanic in town needed help, so I got an apprenticeship. The old owner passed away two years ago, and it got sold to another company, but I kept my job, just with a new boss. He's a hardass, but he spends most of his time off-world, so as long as I keep fixing tractors, it's okay. But I could open my own shop one day. Go independent. Then make enough cash to get offworld. Send money back home."

"Where would you go?"

"Somewhere with beaches. Yisa? It has beaches, right?"

"So I hear," I said, laughing. Everyone wanted to visit the resort world.

"But then - I don't know. Perhaps a mining planet. They always need mechanics."

"They do," I agreed.

I pulled a stone from my pocket and started turning it over in my hand, tossing it up and catching it.

"What do you do for fun?" I asked, "When it's just you? And not work? And not babysitting?"

He paused, thinking. "I play jenball with Tim from the diner. And I fix up some old computers. Or babysitting. And if I'm honest, I actually don't *hate* playing with my sisters. Just don't ever tell them that,"

I smiled, "My lips are sealed,"

I scuffed at a rock on the ground, and then I asked, "Hey, I thought I saw some kids skipping school the other day."

"Oh yeah?" He asked, "Are they still doing that? We used to head down to the creek."

"The creek? There's an *actual* creek at Keita's Creek?"

"Actually, no. There *was* a creek. Now, it's just a creek bed, but it makes the best jenball court in town. It's basically the most popular hangout in town - but only if you're invited."

"And were you invited?"

"Only once," he said sheepishly.

I laughed, and he grinned a little self-consciously. He shrugged and then pointed to the sunset, "Hey, we might spot an aurora tonight."

"Isn't there an aurora here every night?"

He laughed, "Well, it's a better view from up here."

As the sun set, the sky shifted to a deep blue, green and purple painted across the sky. The clouds were lit from behind. The stars shimmered, and distant planets sparkled.

"It's worth the view up here, isn't it?" Jon said softly.

"It is," I said. My mind drifted to Mila, wishing she had been here to experience it.

Mila and I drove home during dusk alongside Jon, who knew the roads. It was dark by the time we got to the farm.

"See you tomorrow night at the dance!" he called to me from his landbike. "Unless I run into you again. I need to deliver some code to Mr Pesce tomorrow, so maybe I'll see you on the road again!"

I laughed, "You might just! Goodnight!" I called back, watching him drive off.

Mila turned to me, beaming, "Good work," she breathed. "He likes you,"

My stomach started flip-flopping, and I wasn't sure if it was because Jon liked me or because Mila had said I'd done a good job.

"We'd better head back in before Mr Larsen sends a search party."

SEVEN

We entered the Ag Store and could see at the front counter that Mr Pesce had his arms folded, mouth drawn. Elin had her hands on her hips and met his gaze. It looked like a standoff.

"I want to reserve the right to refund if this product if faulty," Mr Pesce said.

"I've told you a million times, Pesce. *No refunds.*" She pointed to the sign at the counter.

"I've been laying this over my crops for weeks, and *nothing* is growing. Your product is faulty."

"You need soil, water and sunlight to grow crops. So if your crops aren't growing, it's nothing to do with the fertiliser you bought."

"But my field is empty!"

"What I hear, Mr Pesce, is that you've got a problem on your farm. Maybe you should talk to your - what did you call them? - 'your help'?"

His look darkened.

Elin, exasperated, threw her hands in the air. "Look, if you don't believe me, get an expert to look at your crops. This has nothing to do with the product you bought from me."

Mila nudged me. "They need an expert to look at crops."

I paled. "Do you mean like we did on Prema?" she nodded. My stomach knotted. I didn't want to deal with slimy Mr Pesce more than I needed to.

"It might be a good chance to see Jon again. Didn't he say he needed to deliver that new code over there today?"

I groaned, but before I could argue back, Mila had stepped forward, clearing her throat.

"Mr Pesce? I couldn't help but overhear that you need a crop specialist? I know we've only met once, but off-world, we specialise in reading soil, so we'd be happy to help-"

"You're Larsen's girls."

"We are independent contractors who happen to be helping Mr Larsen at the moment," Mila said, keeping her cool.

"No, I'll get an expert; thank you very much."

"We've just come offworld from-"

Elin put a hand to her forehead as if to ease a blazing headache that had struck. "For Hardhugadr's sake, Pesce! *I'll* hire them.

I'm going to get the girls to help me deliver the rest of this fertiliser. And when they are at your property, if they *happen* to see what's wrong with your crops, you can pay them fifty credits for their time."

We did need all the credits we could get. I shrugged, "Sounds fair."

Mr Pesce pursed his lips. "I can't stop you from working for Elin - but when you enter my land, not a toe goes outside the path I assign you."

Elin rolled her eyes behind him but then clapped her hands. "Excellent. Everyone wins. Girls, the fertiliser is in the back."

Mr Pesce paid for the fertiliser and then headed back to his own truck. Mila shoved the double doors that read "staff only". Out the back was, unsurprisingly, even more warehouse. In this back section was even more of everything. If the front had three bags of something, this section had fifty. Mila found the bags of fertiliser and threw a bag over her shoulder. I found a trolley and heaved a few bags on there before wheeling it over to the dandelion-yellow truck. The stench burned my nostrils, but I'd spent a lot of my childhood working with compost and fertiliser, so while it burned, I knew it was part-and-parcel with farming.

Elin joined us a few minutes later, referring to a logbook, muttering to herself. Seeing us with the fertiliser, she sighed.

"I must apologise for Mr Pesce. He's the most odious human on the planet."

She pointed to the truck parked in the warehouse. "He's ordered fifteen bags. I don't know what kind of drama he will start if he thinks there is something wrong with his fertiliser. For goodness' sake, we all know it's just what's in these fertiliser bags, and it's not worth all this fuss."

We finished loading the truck, and we climbed in. As Elin drove out of the warehouse into the sun, she unwound a window, letting the breeze hit us and turned on the radio. The cab was filled with bright music. She started singing an upbeat song I'd never heard. "This was my favourite band when I was your age," she called over to us as we left town and started driving past the rows of wheat fields.

"Is this band from Birumu?"

She shook her head, "Oh, no! They were from Yisa! I studied at the university there for a few years. Such a wild couple of years." She grinned, "Being off-world for the first time away from my parents is a wild time-" then she turned to us with a wink, " -but I suppose you know *exactly* what I mean."

Mila hid a half-smile but then called, "What did you study?"

"Oh, a bit of everything. I wasn't very focused then. I did art. And business. And law. I think I changed every few months, but somehow the university gave me enough credits in *something* to pass. My parents wanted me to study politics to follow in my father's footsteps. But it was the last thing I wanted to do! I didn't think that sitting in meetings arguing in circles ever got anything done! I wanted *real* action, *real* change."

"Sounds like you had a rebellious few years," Mila grinned.

Elin laughed. "I don't think I ever grew out of them! I went to my share of protests, of course. There was a housing shortage at the time, so we protested. Rights for sentient robots. Laws to punish corporations from damaging planets any further."

I nodded at that. I had seen the damage to Prema that corporations with one goal - profit - could cause to the environment. Prema's entire ocean was missing because the corporation had damaged the planet so badly.

"How did you end up running an Ag store?" Mila asked.

Elin laughed. "Well, life just kind of pulled me here. I told you that I wanted real action, not just meetings. So I spent a few years as a farm hand with Katie - Arvie's wife. I loved the physicality of getting my hands in the soil and making something grow. At the time, I knew there were problems with robo-farming. We all did. But I didn't think I could do anything about it. The system was too big."

"But then?"

"Well, things changed when Katie got sick. Arvold started doing their organic farming and struggled to get any supplies on-world to make it happen. The previous owner of the Ag Store made a big song and dance about how hard it was to ship things here. And I thought, *for Hardhugadr's sake, I could do a better job*. I figured that I had the money, and after that expensive education, surely I could work it out. So I just bought the store and started stocking the supplies Katie and Arvold needed."

"What did your parents think when you bought the Ag store?"

"Oh, my mother *hated* it. Every time she met me, she asked me how my 'little shop' was doing. Just to spite her, I bought a few more stores on other planets, and now I've got five stores. Not that she's still around to judge me," she said, self-consciously touching the diamond pins in her hair. I wondered if they were a dig at her mother, too.

"We might not *think* we have the power to make change. But sometimes, our strengths come in ways we didn't expect. I was powerless to stop Katie's sickness. But I *could* buy an Ag business and stock supplies she needed to run a new kind of farm. I can't change the whole galaxy, but I can impact one farm. One planet. One sector of space."

She flicked on the indicator, and it made a loud *click-clack-click*. She pulled down a driveway. A carved wooden sign over the drive read *'Pesce Produce'*. We'd arrived.

Mr Pesce's farm looked normal from the outset, but it *felt* a little off. There were wide fields with rows of lettuce, kale and carrots and a large white farmhouse with thick columns, which reminded me of the art gallery back on Tevinter. Long cobb-brick buildings around the property looked like warehouses, but as we walked closer, I realised they must have been dorms for the workers. There were neat paths between the buildings and the fields, where rows of workers silently worked. Unlike every other farm I'd visited, there was no hint of chaos - no one walked off the path, no one laughing or singing, and no chickens or dogs running amok. The workers in their matching pale cotton shirts set about doing their manual tasks of weeding, planting or watering in neat rows.

Mr Pesce made a point of greeting us and reminding us not to leave the path. I was tempted to kick a stone into the grass as a quiet act of rebellion.

We headed to one of the warehouses, and Mr Pesce pointed to where we needed to stack the fertiliser in a far corner. Some workers nearby were washing lettuce, once again with the look of not quite comprehending the world around them that I'd seen at Elin's store.

"Should I get started transporting this fertiliser while you begin your, er, consultation?" Mila asked.

"Thanks," I said, and Mila headed back to the truck.

Pesce led us down to one of the fields that were covered in fertiliser but had nothing growing in it.

"This is the offending fertiliser," he said, crossing his arms. I looked at the field, assessing it. From this perspective - good soil, bright sun and water, things *should* be growing in this field.

But I also knew that the fertiliser couldn't be doing anything to *prevent* anything from growing. Nearby, a row of men in pale shirts dug holes and watered them.

If I were going to continue my ruse of being a soil consultant and not a biokin, I needed to look like I was doing more science than I was. Out of my bag, I pulled a piece of piping I'd borrowed from the Ag Store. It had a glass tube that I stuck into the soil, and I plugged some cords into my navcomm in a show of setting up my 'testing equipment'.

"It will take a few minutes to calibrate," I said, stealing a phrase I'd heard Mila use once.

Mr Pesce rolled his eyes and, after waiting impatiently for a moment, marched over to the nearby workers to check their work. I settled into the soil to meditate to find out what was wrong in the field. The soil was cool beneath me, and I could hear birds chirping overhead. Across the field, Pesce was yelling at one of the workers whose shirt was on inside out. I bit my lip, trying to not let him rile me, and I focused on my task.

I found a small weed in the dirt and tucked my fingers around it, connecting with it. I closed my eyes, ready to sink into the surrounding network, to feel the tiny seedlings across the field. It lit up in my mind, but instead of the connection with the plants about me, I could sense nothing.

My heart quickened. Was it possible that my powers had diminished even *further*? How was that possible? The connection

I'd had my entire life with plants was now severed. My stomach twisted. What was going on?

I focused again on the weed in front of me, and it lit up fluorescent in my mind. I frowned. I could connect with *this* plant - but why not any others in the field? And then I opened my eyes. I marched over to the next row of upturned soil where the plants should have been growing. And I started digging across the row.

There were no seeds here.

And I looked back at the workers, watching them. They were digging holes. Filling them in. Watering them. *But they hadn't planted any seeds.*

"What is it?" Elin asked, shading her eyes against the sun.

"I - I think the workers have, um, forgotten to plant the seeds."

Elin rolled her eyes. "Oh, Heavens above".

I pulled out my science equipment from the ground and tucked it back into my bag.

"This is going to be an awkward conversation."

Mila had nearly completed loading the fertiliser into the warehouse as we headed back to help her. I grabbed a bag, and Mila picked up the other half, which we carried over to the warehouse.

"Did you get it all sorted?" Mila asked.

"This is the strangest farm I've ever been on," I said by way of answer. Mr Pesce was in a state, red-faced, digging up the field for any evidence of seeds planted and screaming wildly at the workers.

"I know what you mean," she said, nodding to the workers sorting the lettuce. "There is a kid over there that keeps staring at my pile of fertiliser like I've brought in a hot apple pie."

As we carried the last bag over, Elin checked her notebook. "Oh, it looks like I made a mistake in all the fuss. There's an additional bag that doesn't need to be in this lot. Pesce will lose it if he thinks I've charged him extra."

She nodded to the boy who was staring at us. It was the same one I'd seen her give the bread to in the store. "Taewin?" she called him over. "Can you set this one aside? I'll account for it next time. I don't want to deal with the headache of taking it back; otherwise, Mr Pesce will think I'm robbing him."

He nodded and started dragging the bag out a side door.

As we headed back to the truck, a humanoid robot stopped us. My jaw dropped. This was the first robot I'd seen on the planet.

"Security assessment," its robotic voice said. The robot has a humanoid torso and four wheels covered in blue and white stripes. I could see Mila stiffen. It was a security bot.

In a mechanical voice, it said, "You are not being monitored. You are free to go."

"Thanks," Mila said with a sigh of relief.

"Happy New Year," it said.

"Happy New Year to you," Elin said. "And just what year is it?"

"Hardhugadr's Dawn 941," the security bot responded.

As we climbed into the truck, Elin said softly, as if the bot could still hear us, "It thinks it's New Year's Day five years ago. I bet it hasn't had a software update in a *long* time."

Mila frowned. "So it's in charge of the prisoners?"

Elin nodded.

"How has the prison board not noticed the bot hasn't been getting updates?"

"Our planet has always had comms problems. If Pesce told them he's manually installing them, they probably don't have the manpower to check. Or he paid someone off."

"But what happens if a prisoner has *ended* their sentence in the past five years?"

Elin averted her gaze.

"Not a lot of prisoners *end* their term here. And I bet that's why. Because the bot thinks it hasn't ended."

EIGHT

Dances at home were one of my favourite events of the year. When I was younger, Sabine and her sisters would visit my house, and we'd weave flowers in each others' hair before the dance. When we were kids, we'd run about the dance hall playing hide and seek and joining for a dance or two if one of our parents cajoled us. Platters of fruit and mead were passed around, while fireflies were strung up in glass jars hanging from a thick white rope, crisscrossing across the roof. As we got older, Sabine taught us to rouge our cheeks with crushed berries, and we built the courage to dance. And then, we just enjoyed dancing, whether anyone was dancing with us or not. We'd spin in circles, laughing and breathless in each other's arms.

I was more than a little excited to see what these dances were like on Birumu. I couldn't stop peeking out the window to see if I could get a glimpse of the Midsummer dance as we drove up in Mr Larsen's truck.

We drove at a snail's pace past the wheat fields but could hear the beating of the drums through the air.

We turned down the driveway at Bees End and spotted the large barn. It was lit up like the sun, and white paper lanterns floated all around it, drifting high into the purple-tinged sky. As I drummed my fingers on my knees, a stupid grin was plastered on my face. Mila, despite herself, laughed with me as we peeked out the window, seeing the crowds milling out outside the barn and the scent of spices and perfumes floating through the air.

We parked and climbed out, adjusting our outfits. I wore the blue lightning bolt dress that Elin loaned me, and Mila was in her yellow waistcoat and trousers. Mr Larsen had somehow found a dashing suit in his wardrobe, which was all black, but with a yellow bow tie. He wore a little lightning pin on his right breast.

Earlier that evening, when Mila walked downstairs, my breath was caught, once again, by her outfit with the yellow waistcoat. Mila usually wore her jumpsuit, covered in oil. But when she pulled on a clean outfit and arranged her hair, she was easily the most beautiful girl in the room.

Mr Larsen opened up the back of the truck and handed out the sparkmelons. He handed one to me, and two to Mila, while he carried in a cloth sack of freshly baked cranberry bread.

As we walked into the barn, we could hear the other instruments in the band burst to life in an upbeat tempo. On the stage, the band consisted of musicians wielding a fiddle, bass, drums and harmonica. Some people were lounging about in front of the band on bales of hay, listening to the music, while others had already started dancing. Elin had picked my outfit well. Women wore long dresses in yellow and blue, with lightning bolts all over them. Men wore suits with gold accents.

To the side was a buffet table serving food and punch, and behind that was an enormous pile of food below an altar of Hardhugadr. Across the barn was what looked like a small funfair. Someone had set up the ring-throwing game coits, which we also had back on Tevinter and a wood-block stacking game where some kids were building a tower trying to prevent collapse. I could see face painting and a small horse for the children to ride. There was also a lamb running about, and another group of kids were trying to guide it toward the dance floor. The whole barn was decorated in brightly coloured lanterns and triangles of gold fabric.

We deposited our sparkmelons on the altar and then looked around the room. I spotted Elin across the barn and waved. She wore a sheer light blue dress with a gold sash about her waist and diamonds pinned in her hair. Mr Larsen excused himself to say hello.

Mila scanned the dancefloor and then said to me, "I need to go and powder my nose," at which she headed to the bathroom. I waited outside, leaning against the wall next to a decorative sculpture made of corn. I was trying to spot Jon, who I was due to meet any minute, especially as I wasn't particularly visible from this angle.

Around the corner of the wall, on the other side of the sculpture, I could hear two men talking.

"Has that little problem been resolved?" one man asked the other quietly.

"Very nearly," said the second voice. "Be patient. These things take time."

"I don't have time," snapped the first voice.

After a moment, the first voice mused, "Who are those girls staying with Mr Larsen?"

"Silly girls from offworld who are playing farmhand."

"Don't underestimate pretty young girls, Mr Pesce. They are in the best position to manipulate everyone." There was silence from Pesce, so the second voice continued, "Don't roll your eyes. It's true. I had a young cousin growing up who lived with me. She always helped with the housework, so everyone loved her. But as we got older, my sister grew pale and sickly. My cousin would keep helping with the housework, host guests to visit with gifts, and follow the doctor's orders to make soup. She loved the attention that came from looking after my beloved sister." And then the voice paused. "But she was poisoning my sisters' morning meal. Day in and day out. For years. But who listens to a child? No one."

"Did she get away with it?"

"... She got what was coming to her."

A chill passed over my skin.

A hand grabbed my arm. I jumped. It was Mila. "You okay?"

"Yes," I said, a little breathless. We walked back toward the main entrance, and I turned to see who Mr Pesce had been talking to. The Evo man, Mr Farrell.

My stomach boiled. *What a creep.*

Before I could tell Mila, I almost fell over Jon and Tim, carrying a large basket of unerberries between them. I shook off the overheard conversation. Farrell and Pesce could wait. I remembered the goal of tonight - to get close to Jon.

"Hi!" I called, grabbed a corner of the basket and helped them place it at the altar. Jon had on a dark blue suit. His shirt had an intricate pattern of lightning bolts embroidered all the way down it. Tim wore a burgundy suit with a gold lightning pin on the collar.

"Ladies!" Jon grinned. "Hello! Mila, you remember Tim?"

Mila's expression showed that she remembered Tim but had no interest in being roped into a double date. I met her gaze and hoped she could read my thoughts. *If I had to play along, she had to.* She plastered a smile on her face, switching like the chameleon I'd seen back on Prema.

"Yes! You own the cafe, right?"

And he blushed, "I don't own it; I just work there," he said, blushing.

Jon pointed to the game of coits at the funfair. "Want to play?"

I nodded and looped my arm through Jon's as we strode towards the games. As I turned to see if Mila was following, Tim surveyed Mila's suit. "Is this your customary dress from your planet--?"

"Sure is," she said in a manner that implied she was not answering any further questions on the subject.

She held out her arm to Tim, who, after hesitating a moment, looped his arm through hers.

"I have to warn you," she teased, "I will probably win at coits,"

"I'm not bad myself," warned Tim with a half smile.

We played a round of coits, and I held my own, getting two rings on the wooden target. Jon's hands were shaking the whole time, so he missed it entirely. Mila got three on target, but Tim did too.

Mila's eyes narrowed and challenged him to another two rounds.

Jon pulled me aside and invited me to see the paper lanterns outside. "Coits is obviously not my strong point," he reddened.

As we stepped outside into the night, a refreshing cool breeze hit me.

"So, how is work going?" I asked Jon.

He shrugged evasively. "I don't really want to talk about it. My boss has become a new kind of unhinged. He's been threatening to fire me unless I somehow perform a miraculous task that has nothing at all to do with my job."

"I'm sorry to hear that," I said.

"Me too. I wish there were other places around here hiring but there just aren't. I need the job so much. For Kem."

"Well, if it helps, I have no doubt you will be able to pull off your miracle."

He smiled weakly.

"Thanks."

We walked on in silence. A few metres away from the barn, a group of people were gathered. They all held paper lanterns, lighting a wick at their base and seeing them drift into the sky. They looked like phosphorescent fish meandering downstream, buffeted by the wind as they rose. A hundred paper lanterns dotted the night sky, bright against the green-and-pink electrosphere.

"What is all this?" I laughed, enchanted.

"They are wishes," Jon explained. "You write your wish on the paper inside the lantern. You light it, and it travels up into the sky. My mum would say that because it's not metal, it goes through the electrosphere, right to Hardhugadr, waiting in the sky. And, if you've been good, he'll grant it."

He handed me a lantern and a pencil with a half-smile.

"And do you believe it?" I asked him.

He shrugged, "Can't hurt,"

I looked at the little paper tail out the bottom of the lantern. What would I wish for? That Evo didn't find us. To save the Ancient One. To have the ship repaired. For Mila to find Bianca.

"What will you wish for?" I asked Jon.

"You're not meant to tell," he said, but then leaned to my ear and whispered, "Cake."

I laughed, "Is that the best thing you can wish for?"

"I'm hedging my bets. I wished for something big in the past, and it never came true. I thought I was asking too much of Hardhugadr. So, I figured that this year, I would make it something a bit more realistic."

I grinned and, inspired by his frivolity, I wrote, *A kiss.*

I folded up the paper so he couldn't see. He held my lantern while I lit the wick. The flame caught on to the wick in a lick, and all at once, the lantern glowed a bright yellow. It started tugging itself towards the stars. "Let go!" Jon cried, and as I did so, it soared into the night sky, turning into little white dots amongst the starry expanse. My wish was with Hardhugadr now.

I held his lantern while he lit his. We watched his wish meet the constellations above us.

We stood by the buffet table, eating cake. It was made of carrot with a honey glaze and served on banana leaf plates. We watched the step-step-step-jump as people danced to the fiddle. The revellers clapped hands, hooked elbows and spun around, laughing and breathless.

I couldn't see Mila anywhere, but I did see Tim now talking to a red-headed girl by the funfair, looking like he was imitating a jenball move. Mr Larsen and Elin were on the dance floor. They were terrible dancers, laughing at themselves the entire time. Mr Larsen kept stepping on Elin's expensive-looking shoes, and his ears reddened every time. When Elin spotted me with Jon, her brows drew together momentarily, but then she turned back to the dance. I also spotted the Evo man, Mr Farrell, lurking in a corner, arms folded, eyes watching Elin and Mr Larsen intently. It gave me the creeps.

"Before I forget, I've got some questions for Mila about the injector coil," he said. "On her ship. It's a *Stargrazer* model, right? I need to know if it's a pre-circan design or post."

"Sure. I'll let her know to drop by." I said, picking at my cake.

"I'm amazed you made it through the electrosphere without damaging more, to be honest. Most people's engines are fried beyond repair. The storm catches onto anything running electric and just zaps it."

"We actually didn't have the engine on," I said, "We were just coasting," I said.

"Huh," he mused, "that explains how you got through without too much damage. But why was your engine off?"

"Oh, we had travelled a long way and were out of power. We had come from Prema," I caught myself. Was I meant to keep that a secret? I imagined Mila wouldn't have even told him that much.

His eyebrows raised. "Prema? That's a week's travel!"

"That's why we were out of power," I laughed.

"Prema - that sounds so familiar," he frowned. "Has it been in the news lately?"

I didn't want to discuss Prema, especially if the conversation led anywhere near Evo. Especially as creepy Mr Farrell was just metres away.

I pretended I hadn't heard him above the music and turned to Jon, suddenly, clasping his hands.

"Do you dance?" I asked, eyes drilling into his.

His cheeks burned as he shifted uncomfortably from foot to foot, "I learned these dances at school...."

"Teach me," I said, pulling him onto the dance floor.

The fiddle burst to life. Partners stamped their feet, spun around and clapped their hands, some partners colliding with others, giggling.

"This dance is the Winemaker," he said, his voice cracking as he tried to remember the moves, "They say that this is the dance you do to create wine."

I nodded, picking up my skirt, ready to dance.

"We clap hands like this," he said, "It's like pulling the grapes from the vine. Then we grab hands and go side to the side - this is us climbing in the barrel - "and then, he said, with a wink, "we spin on the grapes," and he hooked his arm around mine and we spun around. As we twirled, it reminded me of spinning like this as a child, and I couldn't help but giggle as we circled around and around. I could see the other dancers around me, red-faced and merry, dancing and laughing. Even Mr Larson seemed to be enjoying himself as he had now more or less learned the moves.

Jon slowed us down out of the spin, and dizzy, I clutched his arm to keep my balance.

I looked into his blue eyes, and he shook his head with a smile, "Keep up, Addi."

The verse began again, and we started clapping hands again. We spun around and around, giggling as we made the turns. The song ended, and gasping for breath, I headed to the side of the dancefloor, looking for something to hold on to in order to stop my spinning head.

"Having fun?" Jon asked. I leaned into him, clutching his forearm as he held me steady. He smelled of peppermint. His eyes sank into mine, and my heart started to race.

I thought about my wish to Hardhugadr. *A kiss.*

His arm was wrapped about mine, and he leaned forward. I could feel his firm muscles beneath his smooth cotton shirt and his breath against my lips.

And suddenly, someone from behind shoved me into Jon. Our lips met briefly and messily as I fell ungraciously to the floor. Jon was thrown back but managed to right himself. From the floor, I spotted Mr Pesce grab Mr Larsen and shove him against a beam.

"You needed to buy *all* the tasia mushrooms in town?" he roared. The band, startled, stopped playing.

Mr Larsen's eyes narrowed, "Yes, I have an operating farm, and I need it for my fields."

"You needed it *all*?"

Mr Larsen levelled Mr Pesce's gaze. "Yes."

"Liar!" Mr Pesce spat.

"What's the matter, Mr Pesce? Regretting your shady little 'business model'?"

"How dare -"

Elin stepped over to him and tried to peel Mr Pesce off Mr Larson. "That's enough -"

"And *you-*" Mr Pesce roared, turning to Elin, "How could *you* sell-"

"You know the rules as well as everyone else. First in, first serve. If I gave people limits to what they could buy, I'd need to do it for everyone. For instance, I would have to place a limit on the water bought during the drought, so *one* person couldn't hoard it all, leaving other farmers dry." Her eyes drilled into his.

Mr Pesce's face was as red as a beetroot now.

One of the nearby men, the size of a tree, pulled Mr Pesce off Mr Larsen, "Take it outside," he growled, "This is a family event."

"This isn't over," Mr Pesce said, eyes narrowing. He shook them off the tree-sized man and stalked out to the parking lot.

The band cautiously resumed playing. Mr Larsen was staring at the floor, jaw tight. Elin straightened Mr Larsen's tie and gave his arm a gentle squeeze. From across the barn, I noticed the Evo man, Mr Farrell, watching them with interest.

I climbed to my feet and said to Jon, "I need some air." Without waiting for a response, I marched off the dancefloor. Jon started to follow me, but one of his sisters called him over, so he paused, and in that moment, I ducked outside. I headed out to the field where we'd lit the lanterns, now empty of revellers. I leaned over my knees and sucked in the air. My hands were shaking.

There was too much going on. Mr Pesce was not going to stop harassing Mr Larsen. And the Evo man was watching Mr Larsen far too closely for my liking. Eyes on him meant eyes on us. Why was Mr Larsen even a suspect in the bombings in the first place? And that awkward half-kiss with Jon. *Oh, Ancient Ones.* That was a mess.

A pebble bounced by my feet. I stood, trying to work out where it had come from. And now — another one! Was someone throwing pebbles at me?

"Psst!" a voice whispered. I turned around, trying to find the pebble-thrower. I looked about behind me, and then I peered at the roof of the barn. Mila's head ducked out, then back again. A pebbled soared in my direction.

"Is that your way of asking for a Mac-Moe rematch?" I called.

"Sure," she called down, "Come on up." She pointed to a nearby water tower.

I hitched up my skirts and clambered up a ladder and onto the roof.

When I made my way over to Mila, she was lying face up on the roof, yellow vest unbuttoned, watching the stars.

"What are you doing up here?" I asked, lying down beside her.

"I needed some quiet," she said, "And I couldn't deal with Tim anymore. He doesn't shut up about the jenball games he's won. So, now, I'm watching the storms," she said, pointing to the sky in the distance, with a storm building.

She handed me a flask of punch, and I took a sip. It burned as I swallowed it. "Is this the same punch as downstairs?" I asked.

"I might have added a little something extra to this one when I powdered my nose."

We sat in silence, listening to the beat of the music below us, watching the storms inch closer. Lightning lit up pockets of the clouds. A layer here, a layer there. Every flash of light revealed a new cloud weaving around the storm system, each lit in a different colour. It was beautiful.

"What have you been doing?" Mila asked.

"Watching Mr Larsen send Mr Pesce packing in front of everyone," I said with a smile. Mila took a sip of her flask and then handed it to me, and I took a draw from it.

"And I danced with Jon."

"Oh! Did he ask you out?" she asked.

My face started burning. At that moment, I didn't want her to know about the half-kiss. I thanked the Ancient Ones that it was dark.

"Oh, you know," I said playfully, "He did invite me to watch Tim play jenball. You think I should go?"

Mila snorted. She rolled on her side, facing me, her hip curving as she curled her body toward me. Her eyes were alight and her curls, not tied back, fell across her cheek. "It's just a matter of time, Addi. You're gorgeous. There's no way he won't ask you out any day now. And then we'll be able to find Bianca. And save your tree."

My heart started pounding loudly in my ears. My mouth was dry.

"You think I'm gorgeous?"

Her cheeks reddened as she gave a half-smile of assent, and her lips parted slightly. Right at that moment, on top of the barn roof, with the storms flashing across the sky, I wanted to kiss her.

I leaned forward. Mila's lips drew closer to mine. My heart pounded in my chest. She bit her lower lip, a line of the silver moon reflected along it. I brushed her hair back from her cheek and leaned closer-

"Addi! Mila!" a voice called across the yard. Mr Larsen. I sharply pulled away, face burning.

Mr Larsen was wandering about the field of lanterns. "Are you girls out here?"

Elin approached Mr Larsen. "Let's try the car park. They can't be far."

Mila didn't move for a moment, eyes watching me curiously.

"We'd better go," I said, climbing to my feet and quickly making my way to the water tower without looking back at Mila.

Is this you granting a wish, Hardhugadr? I much preferred the Ancient Ones as Gods, thank you very much.

I remembered her smooth lips parting. The curve of her shoulder. Her hair falling about her face. My heart pounded in my ears. I shook my head. Mila was my friend. I didn't want to complicate our friendship. It would be a very awkward journey to the next solar system if things went wrong. And in the back of my mind, I couldn't help remembering Sabine and the almost-kiss that became nothing. Just a flight of fancy for an evening. I didn't want to be that again. I focused on climbing down the water tower, rung by rung, inhaling the cool night air to recollect myself.

NINE

S he smelled of vanilla. Mila's hair tickled my neck as she leaned into me and kissed me, lips soft, breath hot. Her tongue darted against mine. My body responded instantly, electric. My heart thundered in my chest. I leaned forward to pull her close, and I -

- I fell out of bed.

Sunlight poured in through the windows. I could feel my cheeks flush as I realised it had been a dream.

Thank the Ancients that Mila was already up and hadn't seen me tumble onto the floor. I was pretty sure I had bruised one of my knees as I landed on the hard floor.

I exhaled slowly. The dream had seemed so real.

My heart was still racing. I couldn't stop thinking about that almost-kiss last night. Did she want to kiss me too? She looked like she wanted to. I wasn't sure. Mila was hard to read on the best of days.

I staggered to the bathroom and had a long hot shower to shake off the dream. As I was pinning up my hair, Mila entered in her workout clothes, covered in sweat.

"Oh, you're up!" she exclaimed.

"Yes!" I stammered. I, all of a sudden, didn't know how to talk to Mila now that I'd had that dream. *Hardhugadr, you are the worst God in existence,* I thought. I turned to pick up my scattered nightdress and towel, so I wouldn't need to face her.

"After lunch, I'm going to head into town to see Jon. I'll say *hi* for you," she said and said 'hi,' like she was breathless.

My dream of Mila immediately came back to me, and I imagined her hot lips against mine again.

"Er - "I said.

"You don't have cold feet, do you? Keep your eyes on the prize, Addi. We will soon be in Evo's network."

Right. *Eyes on the prize.* Whatever I might be feeling for Mila, it wasn't important. The important thing was getting close to Jon, so we could find Bianca. And we'd be one step closer to rescuing the Ancient One on the Evo spacestation.

"No, of course. I am fine," I said.

"We've got a mission to stick to. Don't get distracted-"

"I'm not-"

"Okay. Good. Then I'll do some recon today. I'll see how much he can code, see how much he likes you...."

My face turned bright red at that point, and Mila started laughing.

"You wouldn't last a day on my home planet, Addi."

I didn't doubt that.

We unloaded the sacks of tasia mushrooms that Mr Larsen had bought from Elin. We stacked them in the corner of the barn, stepping over Sola, who had planted himself right in the doorway in a patch of sun. Electricity rippled over him, and I bet he'd be on the hunt soon.

"Should I take one of these sacks to the kitchen?" I asked Mr Larsen.

"Oh, these mushrooms cannot be eaten," Mr Larsen said. "They're toxic to humans. Great for fertiliser, though!"

We finished unloading the sacks, and Mr Larsen headed back into the house, and we remained to keep threshing the wheat for another hour. I smacked the bag against a stone block again, arms aching.

I knew a lot about mushrooms. I'd spent a lot of time learning about them with Perse at home. I was almost - *almost* - a qualified healer. If I headed back to live on my planet (now a distant prospect), I'd take over Perse as the senior village healer. And I'd always been taught that no part of a plant would go to waste. And while fertiliser wasn't a waste entirely, I wanted to see if there was a more useful part of the mushroom.

I headed over to the sack of mushrooms and peered inside. The mushrooms were about the size of my hand and had a reddish colour but had yellow stripes on the cap. On our planet, these were called Grensa mushrooms, not Tasia.

"These mushrooms are used in ceremonies with the Elders back on my planet," I mused aloud. "They are only poisonous if you eat the cap raw. The stems can be used if you dry them and grind them into powder. They are a relaxant."

Mila stopped threshing and walked over, and peered inside the sack. "To help you sleep?"

"Well, to make you... open," I said, thinking of the ceremonies I'd seen back on Nimbaii, where the Elders would set aside an evening to meditate. "You connect with the Ancient Ones. Open to the universe. Calm."

"You mean compliant? Kind of like *all* of Mr Pesce's farmhands?"

"... Now that you mention it... yes?"

"That's interesting," Mila said, returning to threshing and was now whacking the wheat a little harder on the stone.

"It is," I said, biting my lip.

I knocked on the doorframe of Mr Larsen's office, where he was musing over his glass panel with the farm map. He was marking up the board.

"News is in - we've got a new electrosphere window coming up tonight just after midnight."

"Oh?" I asked, surprised. "Do we need to load the crates?"

He shook his head. "No, it's only a short window. Five minutes. Mostly good for calling the crates back to the surface. Or for sending comms off-world."

"Right," I was relieved. "Do you want us to do anything?"

"No, I'll just program in the signal to the crates to return from orbit."

"Hey, do you need anything from town? If I can borrow the landbikes, I'd like to return our outfits to Elin."

Mr Larsen's ear reddened a little at Elin's name. "No, I am fine. Thanks. After that drama with Mr Pesce last night, I think staying out of town for a few days is in my best interest."

"Right. Sure. Okay," I said. "Well, I'll be back in a few hours."

"I'll be on the tractor watering the east fields."

"Don't stay in the sun too long."

Mr Larsen grinned at that but didn't say anything.

Elin's house was several degrees cooler than outside, which was like wading through an oven. We sat in her sitting room that overlooked her garden with the floor-to-ceiling glass walls. Large abstract paintings and bookshelves decorated the remaining walls. She served icy sparkmelon drinks in gold-rimmed glasses.

I sat on the sofa, sipping the drink carefully, then placed it on the glass table, not wanting to spill any on her sofa.

"Did you enjoy the dance?" Elin asked. "You looked magnificent!"

"Thank you - all thanks to your dress! I don't really have anything like that," I explained, handing her the folded outfits that Mila and I had borrowed. "On my planet, this is mostly what we wear," I said, tugging at my dress, which had repairs and patches from years of use, of when I'd climbed a tree and torn the dress, to sit by the fireside in the evening repairing it, while Mum sang, or told stories from her childhood. My dress looked quite inadequate compared to Elin's silks.

"That's what I love about meeting people from new planets," Elin said, "You bring a new culture and new ideas. And those experiences are woven into the very threads you wear. I love that this dress tells the story of your culture."

"I suppose I'd never thought of it that way," I admitted.

"And I saw you even learned some of the dances," she beamed.

"I did! Although, I still need some practice!"

I remembered during the dance getting bumped by Mr Pesce, and he marched over to confront Mr Larsen.

"You were really brave confronting Mr Pesce," I said.

"Oh, him!" she said dismissively. "He's just a gnat. He'll get what he deserves one day."

"Why does he hate Mr Larsen so much?" I asked.

She sighed and put her drink on the table, wringing her hands. "You would know about what happened to Katie - Arvie's wife? With the wheat?"

"I pieced it together. She got sick right from Evo wheat?"

Elin nodded. "Arvold tried to ban Evo wheat from being grown on the planet. He had a petition, but there was one deciding vote - Mr Pesce. Pesce thought Arvold was trying to destroy his business - a self-centred fool. But Pesce had the money to change a few minds. So, the proposal was overturned. And poor Arvie got the news the day Katie died. He's never forgiven Mr Pesce. Or himself."

A shiver ran down my spine.

"Of course, Arvie couldn't change the planet, but he could control his farm. They had shifted to organic seeds when they found out why she was sick, of course. And ever since, he's been trying to support other people getting sick by giving them an alternative food source. But it's not been easy."

My chest was heavy.

"I'm so sorry," I said, not sure to who I was apologising.

Her eyelids were thick with tears, and she said suddenly, "Let me take these dresses upstairs."

Elin grabbed the package with the dresses and, eyes fixated on each stair she climbed, moved upstairs like in water.

I heard her open the door to the closet but then stay silent for a really long time. There was a muffled sob through the walls.

I stood, looking for a distraction from the heaviness that now weighed on me. At the nearby bookshelf, I pulled a tome off the shelf and leafed through a few pages. But then the book's weight shifted in my hands. The middle of the book had a hole carved in it. And inside was paper money stuffed into it. Reams of it.

I closed the book and checked another - again, money jammed into the pages. *What was this?*

From one of the pages slid out a ream of paper, which had a handwritten note, like a shopping list someone would take to Elin's store. The letters were written perfectly formed, like a child copying from a schoolbook.

It read:

Elin -

Hoe drill
Earth auger
Lemon balm
Planter.

And then, I looked at the first letter of each word on the list. It spelled 'HELP'.

My heart dropped, and the all-too-familiar sensation of overwhelm crept in. Like when the Ancient One asked me to help it escape Evo.

The tap ran for a moment. Elin's footsteps were back on the stairs. I slammed the note back in the book and squeezed it back on the bookshelf.

As she reached the landing, I noticed her makeup was reapplied. I held up the empty glasses, "Shall I take these to the kitchen?"

"Oh, lamb. That's kind, but don't be silly. I will get to them shortly. Now, where were we?"

I sat back down, perched on the edge of the seat. "I think we were talking about Evo."

"Oh yes, of course. Very sad. And, of course, they've become increasingly cemented into the planet now."

"They seem to have a big operation here," I agreed.

"Yes, and forgive me if this is none of my business, but I think it's worth you being careful around Evo people. They might try to get close to you to try to hurt Arvie."

"Oh!" I said, "Of course. I am very careful. I don't think I've even spoken to Mr Farrell at all."

"I don't mean Mr Farrell. I mean Jon."

"Jon?" I echoed. "*Jon* Jon?"

"Yes. A few years ago, the garage where he works was bought by Evo. It kept the same name, of course, but all the locals know it's an Evo outfit. Helps them manage the tractors with all those code deliveries."

Jon worked for Evo.

And Mila was with Jon right now.

Asking him to hack into Evo.

"I need to go," I said, the glass slipping from my fingers.

TEN

I ran. Out of Elin's house. Onto the main street. The heat radiating off the buildings was oppressive. My feet were like lead. I skittered on some loose gravel as I raced around the corner. I could see the garage, the doors open wide.

I ran into the garage, the cool of the workshop hitting me immediately.

"Hello?" I called out. I couldn't see anyone. Piles of machine parts were stacked about the garage, and it felt like a graveyard. The computer with the lines of computer drives was lined up, with the code blinking away on the screen. My cheeks burned, looking at the little datadrive with the old Evo label.

I walked to the back of the garage, past the little kitchenette, checked the bathroom, and out a back door to a grassy laneway. "Hello? Jon? Mila?" I looked closer at the grass, and it looked like the grass was bent. As if something heavy had been dragged through it.

I ran back into the garage, panic rising in my chest, "*Mila?*"

There was a boy there, standing, staring at me. I jumped. It was the boy Elin had given the bread to. Taewin.

He picked up a package on the bench I'd not noticed before, labelled *Pesce*.

"Have - have you seen Jon?" I asked, my voice unnaturally high.

Taewin shook his head, "No." He paused for a moment and said skittishly, "Thank you for not mentioning what you saw with Elin."

"It's fine," I said distractedly. I wasn't sure what he meant, but I didn't have time to think about it. I had bigger problems to work through.

He left, and I was alone again in the shop, desperately trying to find traces of Mila. My mind whirred over and over: Jon worked for Evo. Mila came to see him here, and now they were gone. I took a long, slow breath out. "Stop panicking, Addi. Think."

Could I have been jumping to conclusions? What if she was back at the farm and Jon was out on a regular errand? The damaged grass in the laneway might well have been Jon's landbike. My hands were shaking, but I knew that I needed to check the farm.

I headed back to Elin's, jumped on the landbike and raced back to Mr Larsen's. The property was silent. The wheat stood tall, unaware that my world was tumbling about me. The cicadas were a constant buzz. I ran through the farmhouse, checking every room. "Mila?" I called to the empty house.

Mr Larsen's office was empty. I looked out a window; across the fields, I could see a plume of dirt rising into the sky as Mr Larson harvested the crop.

I headed up to our room to see if Mila was there. I imagined her shaking her head. "I can look after myself, Addi." But it was empty. I swore at Mila's perfectly tucked-in bed and her stupid, neat dresser.

I headed out to the barn and even checked the *Scout*. The ship was cool inside, and my footfalls echoed across the metal.

"Mila?" I called, opening the door to her spartan bedroom. I even managed to open the hatch to engineering and call down. Nothing.

Exhausted and shaking, I curled up on my bed on the ship. Tears welled up in my eyes. I remembered the last time I lay here, crying silently, trying to comprehend the universe I'd stepped into. Everything seemed new and terrifying. So far from my home. The forest. From Lian. Perse. And while I still didn't understand a lot of things, Mila was always there to explain. She was patient. And strong. And smart. And made this universe feel not so scary.

Ancient Ones, how would I find Mila without *her* to help me?

I didn't know the first thing about where to start. I couldn't drive a ship or use any comms. I didn't even have my stupid powers, not that they even worked anymore. I was just a lost biokin girl trapped on a planet that was devoid of anything but sun and wheat.

There was a sinking feeling in my gut that perhaps Jon had realised who Mila was because I'd let slip that we'd come from Prema. Or maybe the alert about us came through during that last break in the electrosphere.

And I sat up and placed my feet on the cool floor of the ship. Mr Larsen had said there was *another* window opening tonight. A comms window. Surely, they would be sending a message right now that they had Mila. And when the window opened, it would send, and then Evo would *know* we were on this planet, and they'd surely send reinforcements. I stood, heart racing. I needed to find Mila before midnight.

I stumbled out of the *Scout*, unsure of my next move. Where could Jon have taken Mila? I had no idea where he lived or where he might take her.

If only the warehouse hadn't been bombed, we would never have even known they were here, and Mila wouldn't have gotten the absurd idea to hack into Evo. *Of course.* The Evo *warehouse.*

But where was it?

I remembered when we were loading the crates the day of the electrosphere, a ship landed to the East of us. Elin has said it was an Evo ship. I looked across the field in the direction of where we'd seen it land. Somewhere in that direction must have been the warehouse.

I tightened the laces on my boots and started to run straight through the field. The soil was uneven and soft but being in the wheat calmed me in a way. Like I was safe. The temperature within the wheat was cooler than outside, so I set a steady pace, mind racing, wheat brushing up against my dress, seeds and dirt clinging to my dress as I ran.

Mila was so determined to find Bianca. But was this the right way to find her? Risking her life? The task was impossible. We were two little leaves about to fall off a waterfall. I had absolutely no power to help her. I thought about the Ancient Tree and its call to me. The image of birds in flight in my mind. *Help*. The fire and burning. The power it gave me.

A fury rose within me. I stopped and glowered at the sky above me. "What power?!" I cried. "You gave me power, Ancient One, but where is it? I haven't been able to move a blade of grass in weeks!"

I started thrashing at the wheat about me, tugging it from the earth, screaming.

"Where is my power? *Where is it?*"

I needed to find Mila. *I needed* to find her. The planet was off its axis until she was with me again. I kept tugging out the wheat and flinging it to the ground in a rage. "I need these powers, Ancient One. How dare you take them from me?!"

Red-faced and furious, I tugged at another stalk of wheat, overbalanced and slipped right over. My face landed in the dirt, and I curled up on the ground, sobbing. My palms were in the soil, and tears fell into the dirt. "*Help me,*" I whispered to the Ancient One. "Help me save Mila,"

And my palms grew hot. A sizzle of electricity behind my eyes. I connected with the field, the wheat turning phosphorescent in my eyes. The stalks of wheat all around me, their life force connected to mine. And then, in a large circle around me, the wheat bowed to the ground, making way for me.

I started sobbing all over again. My powers were back.

"Mila," I whispered. "I'm coming."

It was dusk. The sky was blue, with hints of purple from the electrosphere. I still had a few hours until midnight. At the end of the field, the warehouse loomed over the crops. An hour ago, I'd sat in the fields and meditated, stretching my awareness as far as I could. I looked for the change in vegetation to show the outline of a large building. The warehouse. I set a beeline for it.

My legs were aching. I grumbled to myself because perhaps it would have been smarter to drive the landbike, but I realised I now had the element of surprise creeping in through the wheat.

The warehouse stood tall over the fields. It was one enormous building. Large mechanical arms connected to the roof, which might open up on cargo delivery days. The walls were thick cement, and I could see cameras pointing all around. There was a landbike parked outside, and from another truck, Mr Farrell unloaded something, pausing to survey the wheat field around him.

My palms were sweating. Why had I come out here on my own, with not even a weapon? How was I going to get to Mila?

There was a rustling in the wheat a few metres behind me. Was someone behind me? Or was it just the wind? My senses were on edge. I ducked, hiding low to the ground.

I started creeping towards the warehouse, but suddenly an alarm started howling around the complex. *Cripes.* Had I tripped some kind of alarm?

My heart started pounding. I started running in the opposite direction, hoping to find cover in the wheat. Mr Farrell's voice roared across the field, "Here for that little thief, are you?"

I started running. I wasn't prepared for a fight. But I ran noisily and stumbled over the wheat, unsure of where to run. I heard the crunch-crunch-crunch of Mr Farrell's footsteps as he leapt into the wheat field after me. I should have been faster, but

I'd been running for hours, and my legs were jelly. I kept weaving through the wheat, my legs burning. Mr Farrell's stomping footfalls kept pace behind me.

He called, "She's over here!" and my blood ran cold because it meant that Mr Farrell wasn't alone in the field. How many people were here searching for me? I didn't slow down.

I wished I could call on the wheat around me for help - but I couldn't stop to connect with them. I took a deep breath and closed my eyes. I exhaled and felt the earth beneath my feet. Left foot. Right foot. Left foot. There was never a moment I wasn't connected to the earth. I focused on the connection with each foot and sent a message to the wheat. "Help!" I cried.

Mr Farrell, behind me, let out a bark. "There's no one out here to help you!" he cried. Then, louder to whoever else was in the field, "She's over here!"

Help me, I called again to the wheat, pouring a blast of my power into the earth, feeling unsteady as heat poured down through my feet into the soil.

The wheat behind me began to lean together and weave. The plants interlocked and created a net which caused Mr Farrell to stumble, slow and then, as the plants surrounded him, the wall was impenetrable.

"What in Hardhugadr's name -?!" he growled, swatting at the wheat. I kept running, every footfall taking me further from my would-be captor. The wheat bent forward and let me pass while strangled cries were behind me. I just need to keep going, lose them in the field and then circle back from a different direction. I kept one foot on the ground, breathing hard.

"Thank you!" I called to the wheat —

- and then someone tackled me into the dirt from the left. My arm was pulled behind my back, the pain tearing through my shoulder; I tried to call on the wheat about me to throw him off, but the pain in my arm racked through my body, and I couldn't see, let alone focus.

"I wish this wasn't you," Jon whispered.

Mr Farrell's boots crunched in the dirt.

"What are you-"

And my world went black.

ELEVEN

I blinked. The warehouse was dark except for a glowing computer monitor in the corner. Mr Farrell was hunched over it, typing. He hadn't noticed that I was awake. I tried to move my arms but could feel the cold metal against my wrists. I was handcuffed. And a rope bound me to a chair. *What in the stars?*

The room we were in was large, with a cement floor and, on the far side, a few empty crates and pallets against the wall. On the far wall was an industrial workbench with a computer on it. There were a few large doors on the walls for hauling cargo and a few smaller doors leading either outside or towards other parts of the warehouse.

To the left was a large coolroom.

I wrestled with my bonds, but they wouldn't budge. Damn. *What kind of rescue was this?* I thought.

Mr Farrell kept ignoring me as he typed, and suddenly the door to the coolroom opened from the inside. I thought for a moment that it was Mila breaking free, but my heart dropped when I saw it was Jon, feet dragging as he carried a tray of food.

Through a sliver of light through the door, I glimpsed Mila's frame, also tied to a chair. But she was drooping over it. Like she'd been beaten. And the door closed, sealing her in darkness.

"She's not responding," Jon reported to Mr Farrell, who grunted and roughly put the food tray on the desk.

Jon strode over to me after noticing I was awake.

"Addison," he said under his breath. "What's going on?"

"What do you mean? *You've tied me up!*" I hissed.

"*I had to*. I told you my boss was asking me to do impossible things. And you know I can't afford to lose this job."

So Mr Farrell was Jon's boss. The one that spent most of his time off-world.

"Surely 'following orders' ends at 5pm at the garage?"

His mouth was drawn. "It doesn't work that way. You know I don't have a choice, Addison."

"Everyone has a choice," I said, eyes drilling into his. He broke away and looked at the floor.

"Mr Farrell says you two are criminals. I've seen the alert. It matches your description."

I shifted uncomfortably. "It's a misunderstanding," I said, "I *worked* for Evo."

"So why did Mila ask me to hack into Evo?"

Fuck.

"I admit, things are complicated," I said, voice wavering. "But we're not the bad guys. I can explain everything-"

His face looked pained. "I can't help you," he whispered. He looked back to Mr Farrell, who was now watching us. "I gotta go."

My heart dropped.

Mila was trapped in a locker. I was tied to a chair. And I didn't know how long I'd been out. The warehouse didn't have any light from outside, so I wasn't sure if night had fallen. I would have been out at least half an hour for them to carry me in and tie me up. Or an hour. Perhaps two? Had the electrosphere window opened yet? Had they sent the comms out to Evo yet?

I tried to connect with the earth around me, but we were on cement. The room had no moss for me to connect to and certainly no dirt. The most dirt in this place was on my dress. I was covered in soil and bits of wheat and seeds. My hair was pulled askew, and I could smell the dirt in my nostrils. A right hero I was.

My chest was tight.

I tugged at the bonds, remembering the last time I'd been tied up. When I was young, Lian, Sabine and I used to play by the river. One summer, we learned magic tricks and put on a show in the village, which kindly humoured the enthusiastic seven-year-olds. We pulled flowers from hats, learned to pick locks, and, in our finale, Sabine would be hung upside down from a tree and work her way out of the dummy knots we'd tied. If only all that was real. It would be wonderful to be able to pick the lock on these handcuffs. It was all well and good, having learned how to pick a lock, but I needed a pin if I was going to get out of these cuffs. A hairpin. A rod. Oh, Ancient Ones, I'd even try a stick right now. Or a piece of wheat. There was wheat all around us in the field–surely, we'd have tracked a piece in with us?

I thought about Mila trapped in the locker. In the dark. Mila didn't do well in the dark. She looked so broken in there. Nothing like the bold, beautiful, unbreakable Mila I knew. She really would do anything to save her sister. Even being beaten by some jerks on a backwater planet just so she could get close enough to this computer to find out where her sister was.

I didn't want all this to be for nothing. It couldn't be.

And the Ancient One didn't give me these powers for no reason.

I closed my eyes and breathed out slowly. There had to be something here I could connect with. Anything. I started to meditate. I slowed my breathing and felt the weight of my body against the chair. The industrial fans whirred above me. The temperature was cold, and the air was full of the smell of wheat. The rope itched about my shoulders, the cuffs tight on my wrists. And as I breathed in and out, a spark twinged as I connected to something. Something *small*. That something prodded me through my dress. A seed caught on my dress, surrounded by dirt. I opened my eyes, stunned. Was it even possible to connect to a *seed*?

I scanned the room. Jon was pacing back and forth to check on Mila. Mr Farrell was hunched over the computer, the blue light illuminating his face, his moustache outlined to make him look more like a devil of the woods than a man.

There was a noise outside, like a stone ricocheting off the metal warehouse wall.

"What's that sound?" Jon asked, marching over to the video screens, peering to see the camera's view outside. There was the sound again - one - two - three stones hitting the walls.

"Someone is out there!" Mr Farrell glowered. "Sort it out! But be back soon. The electrosphere will be open in fifteen minutes, and we need to get this message out."

The electrosphere would open in *fifteen minutes*. I had to escape before then.

Jon picked up a taser off the bench and, with a last look at the vid screens to see if he could spot anyone around the warehouse or hiding in the wheat fields, he headed to the exit, face drawn.

I closed my eyes and focused on the seed in my dress. I exhaled and connected with it in my mind. It was glowing brightly in my vision. I imagined Mila in the coolroom hanging over the chair and that every second wasted was a second close to Evo finding out that we were here.

"Help me," I whispered to it. And in my mind, electricity pulsed from me through to the seed, and it sprouted a thick stalk. The perfect lock pick. "Oh, Ancient One, I promise I'm coming for you," I whispered, thanking the creature who had granted these powers. Even if they were a little flaky.

I wriggled until I could grab the stalk and negotiate it into the lock. I threaded the wheat into the handcuffs. The stalk started to bend as I put it in the lock. *Hecking heck.* It was going to be too weak. I needed something stronger to lever the lock inside the cuffs. *Come on, little one!* I begged. I gritted my teeth and connected with the wheat, pouring in my energy. *Stay strong like an oak tree!*

I could feel it strengthen in my fingers, growing firmer as I poured my energy into it. I levered the lock in the handcuffs - to the left, now under and up - and they snapped open. The handcuffs fell from one wrist. I grabbed them with my free hand so they wouldn't make a noise and alert Mr Farrell that I was free.

But his attention shifted between the clock on the wall and his fingers slamming against the keyboard. He needed to finish what he was writing before the window opened. And I needed to stop him.

Heart racing, I silently pulled the handcuffs from my other wrist and began working at the ropes. They slithered away from my skin and fell to the floor. I peeled off my boots so I could walk silently. I tiptoed towards the coolroom where Mila was held. I wrapped my fingers around the door. I grabbed the handle, thicker than my hand, and opened it, but the hinge let out an unearthly wail.

Mr Farrell's eyes snapped to me.

"You little-"

He grabbed the other taser and started racing toward me. Heart thumping, I bolted towards another doorway nearby. Wrenching it open and stumbling inside, I found myself in a long storage room with rows of goods to be shipped off-world. Sacks of wheat, like the ones Mila and I had packed by hand, rolls of hay and tubs of mushrooms growing in soil.

I picked a direction at random and started running through the rows, trying to find somewhere to hide.

Shit. Shit. Shit. My mind circled about, over and over, unable to do anything but run. Mr Farrell wrenched open the door, and I immediately crouched to the floor, hiding. I was behind the sacks of wheat. The smell of it reminded me of Mila. Mila, who used to hum songs from Naas as she threshed the wheat but would be silent as soon as I asked about it. Mila, who would pick out seeds from my hair with a half-smile. Who I still yearned to kiss on a rooftop. Mila was now limp and bound on a chair in the cold room. I exhaled slowly. Getting killed would mean I couldn't help Mila.

"How in Hardhugadr's name did you get out of those handcuffs, you little snake?" Mr Farrell goaded from across the warehouse.

I began crawling along with the stacks of wheat to get further from him. As I crawled, something dug into my waist. A set of stones. My Mac-Moe winnings. It was something I could use. It wasn't much, but it might buy me some time.

"I know all about you two. Sneaking in the Evo space station. Sneaking out with confidential information. They thought because you're young girls that you can't be dangerous. But I know that young girls are the most dangerous of all," he said, footfalls working towards where I hid. "And you need to be held accountable. That's something I can help with," he turned on his taser, and it crackled loudly.

My body jumped, my skin a wave of goose pimples. I breathed out as silently as I could, and I crawled down another row.

"Come out, come out, wherever you are," he sang and then chuckled. "But let's be honest, girl. You're here all alone. Without any weapons."

His shoe squeaked in the row next to mine, so I grabbed a stone from my pocket. I flung it down the aisle as far as I could so the noise clattered on the other side of the warehouse.

"Oh ho!" he said, "Now I've got you!" and his shoes pattered to where the stone had landed.

As I kept crawling, I found myself next to a set of tubs filled with soil, with tasia mushrooms growing from the holes in the tubs. If I could get out of the aisles and hide within the cargo, I could buy myself time to think. To work out how to save Mila.

I squeezed myself into the gap between the tubs, but as I crawled my way in on my side, the stones in my pocket fell onto the concrete. Click. Clack. Clack. I froze.

It was as if a beacon had been set off.

Mr Farrell's shoes thundered towards me. I wriggled further in. Soil tumbled out of the tubs as I wriggled by, covering me in clumps and streaks of dirt.

Mr Farrell's footfalls were now right behind me, and I heard taser fire whip above my head. I jerked and kicked over a few tubs, the contents spilling everywhere. Soil and tasia mushrooms were all about me.

"Get up!" Mr Farrell cried, and when I didn't, he fired the taser into the pile of tubs. A laser shot sizzled past my head. My body was soaked with sweat. I didn't have any other options.

Hands shaking, I stood, raising my palms in the air.

"There's a good girl," he growled, holding the taser at me. He stepped closer, his feet stamping through the spilled dirt and mushrooms. "Now, down on your knees," he said, gesturing with his taser, "Oh no - keep your hands up! I can't have you reaching for some secret weapon."

I lowered myself to my knees, sinking into the soil. It was cool and moist. My knees squished straight into a wet mushroom. It reminded me of hunting mushrooms with Perse. And I remembered my forest. And of the Ancient One that I needed to save. Of my powers.

"I don't need to reach for a weapon," I said, eyes meeting his.

He looked at my bare hands in the air and then at his taser. "One move, and I'll tear your kneecaps off. I get paid as long as you're alive, sweet-cheeks."

"I don't need to reach for a weapon," I repeated. "Because I *am* the weapon."

He started to scoff, but at that moment, my powers surged to life. My body buzzed with electricity, and I connected with the soil around me. With the mushrooms. In my vision, the connection between the plants in the soil lit up like fireflies in my mind. *Stop him,* I begged, and the mushrooms about his feet ballooned and swelled, becoming enormous. They wrapped around his shoes and pinned him in place. They didn't stop, and the stems wrapped up his legs, around his waist and held him tight. As they twisted about his arms, I stepped forward and grabbed the taser. I pointed it at him. The mushroom caps bloomed about his face, and the toxic mushroom spores sat just inches from his face.

"Stay really still, Mr Farrell. Don't you know that tasia mushrooms are toxic to humans?"

"I - what - you?!" he stammered.

I walked backwards towards the door, pointing the taser towards him, and as I reached the door, I shoved it open with my hip. I slammed the door back against it, where I finally exhaled. Hands shaking, I found a piece of wood from a pallet and wedged it into the door. I then ran to the other side of the room and did the same for the door Jon had left by. The threat of a poisonous mushroom would only hold him for so long, and then the spongy fungi wouldn't be too hard to escape from unless he really did breathe in the spores. Which wasn't impossible.

I raced toward the coolroom, keenly aware that every second was a second closer to the electrosphere window opening. With that, Mr Farrell's message to Evo announcing that we were on this planet.

I hauled open the door, and the hinge howled again, and I smacked straight into Mila, who shoved me to the ground. "Addi?!" she cried in surprise, "I thought you were Jon!" and then promptly lost her balance and then toppled on top of me. Our eyes met, and my heart started drumming in my chest like a band. Her lips were just moments from mine. But her words echoed in my mind: *Eyes on the prize.*

"What are you doing here?" Mila asked.

"Um? Rescuing you?"

She clambered up and held a hand out for me. "Good job," she said, pulling me up.

"But I saw you - you were tied up -"

"Always let them underestimate you," she said, winking. "And never let them check for knives."

I leaned forward and pulled Mila into a hug. "Mila," I breathed, "I'm so glad you're okay!" She wrapped her hands around my back gently and held me for a moment. I breathed in Mila, one breath. Two. My heart finally returned to a normal beat.

"Thanks for coming to rescue me, Addi," she said softly.

"Always."

There was a banging sound at the main doorway. Jon trying to get back in. Mila peeled away from me, back to business. "Where's Mr Farrell? And Jon?"

"Elsewhere," I said because it was too long to explain. And then I remembered the time. "We need to hurry. Mr Farrell has prepared a message to Evo, and it's about to send when the electrosphere opens."

"How long do we have?"

"It's any moment now!"

We raced over to the computer. Mr Farrell had left the computer running, so Mila sat down and began searching through messages and reports.

She highlighted one that read "ALL STAFF ALERT", and it was from Mr Vulant, Head of Innovation at Evo. Richard. The man we'd met on Evo, who took a sample of my blood to see if I had some markers. Whatever that meant. I shivered. Mila quickly scanned the document but announced, "Nothing. It just says to alert them if they see us. Our names. A description. Doesn't say why. They want us alive, which is nice news."

"Three minutes," I said, eyeballing the clock on the wall.

There was a banging sound against the warehouse doors, like metal against metal. I turned to look through the video screens. Out by the fields, Jon had found a forklift and was now ramming it against the door to try to break the lock. "Hurry!" I whispered to Mila.

She opened up his messaging system and the report about us sitting in the outgoing messages folder. She quickly scanned the message, then hit delete on the queued outgoing message, and a little icon showing that the delete was processing was whirring on the screen. "Hurry up," Mila hummed. "How big is the freaking report? Just delete already -"

And then a bomb went off.

TWELVE

F ire engulfed the room. While the crates were empty, they'd been wood, so it only took moments for us to be surrounded by fire as they started catching alight. The warehouse had a hole blown in the side from the bomb. I could see people rushing outside but couldn't see their faces through the inferno.

Mila had clocked the explosion a split second before I did and had pushed me back from the blast. Her arm was wrapped about my back, shielding me from the fire, as we huddled in the warehouse. We kept as far away from the flames as possible and low to avoid the smoke. Someone outside had already set water cannons onto the warehouse, and the fire was being doused.

"Addison! Mila!" called a voice from outside. Elin. It was Elin.

The water had cleared a path to the exit, and the wood I'd used to jam the exit door had crumbled away in ash. We fell out of the door into a crowd who were holding a fire hose. Elin raced up to us.

"Oh, you poor girls!" Elin cried. "Are you okay? I was so worried when you ran off!"

"Where is Jon? And Mr Farrell?" I asked, looking about. The only other people here were the people fighting the fire. All with pale cotton shirts. Mr Pesce's slaves.

Elin shrugged. "Not here."

She fetched us some water from her canteen and checked us over for wounds from the explosion. A few bumps and bruises, but we were okay.

"Everyone got here so fast," I murmured as Elin tucked us into the backseat of her truck.

"It's a small community," she said, "We need to help each other in times like these."

I wrapped my arms around Mila, who tucked her head against my neck.

"I'm so glad you're safe," she whispered to me.

"Me too," I whispered back. I grabbed her hand, wrapping my fingers around hers. I dozed, the smell of wheat, smoke and Mila in the air as Elin drove us back to the farm.

"Girls!" Back at the farmhouse, Mr Larsen ran up to the car. "Are you okay? You didn't come home, and then there was a bombing across town-"

"They're fine, Arvold," Elin said, putting a hand on his shoulder. "Just got into a bit of an incident with Evo, that's all."

Mr Larsen raised his eyebrows. "With Evo? What have you girls got to do with Evo? That Mr Farrell wasn't trying to get information from you about me, was he?!"

I flushed, "No, Mr Larsen, it had nothing to do with you,"

"Then what happened?" he asked.

"We actually have our *own* trouble with Evo," I said, and Mila tugged at my arm for me to be silent. I leaned over to her and whispered in her ear, "Trust me on this."

She looked annoyed but, to my surprise, remained silent. I remembered one of the first things that drove me to trust Mila was that we had a common enemy in Evo. *The enemy of my enemy is my friend.*

"I think you better come inside," said Elin, and we headed into the farmhouse.

Mila and I sat on the old, creaky sofa with hot chocolates. Mr Larsen sat in the old armchair. Elin dragged over one of the chairs from the kitchen table.

"So," I started. "I am a biokin. I can talk to plants."

I explained what had happened to me when I left my planet and visited Evo. How I met Mila. I didn't mention that the

Ancient One had given me new powers, but I *did* explain that they'd run an experiment on my biokin abilities and that they were searching for a specific biokin. They even took some of my blood to check. Mila grudgingly explained how her sister went missing when she got a job at Evo. And about when we landed here, we thought there was a chance we could access their system and find where Bianca was. That is why we'd befriended Jon, not realising he effectively worked for Evo.

"So that's why Evo is interested in *us*," I explained. "We were hoping to come to this planet to lie low for a while."

"But we didn't expect to land on a planet where people were bombing Evo warehouses, which led them to look closer at this planet." Mila shrugged. "I still don't even understand why that's been happening."

"I think I do," I said. "But I think the best person to explain it all is Elin."

Everyone turned to Elin, who paled. "I'm sorry?"

"You're helping to bomb the Evo warehouses, right?"

Her mouth hung open a little.

"Don't get me wrong - I think what you've been doing is a kind thing. But it was bad timing for us." She remained silent, so I continued. "Everyone thought the warehouses were being bombed because someone wanted to stop them shipping the wheat *off-world*. Which is why you were the suspect," I nodded to Mr Larsen.

"But the bombing was to destroy the drones to interrupt the *deliveries* that Evo was making. Of the tasia mushrooms to Mr Pesce. Which worked. And that's why Mr Pesce was in your store trying to buy your whole stock because he couldn't get them from Evo."

"What does that-" Mila started.

"Mr Pesce discovered that tasia mushrooms, when prepared correctly, can be used to subdue people. He'd been drugging his prisoners. So, they were so compliant that they didn't realise they should not have their sentences extended. And then one day, a couple of them stopped eating the food he gave to them and managed to organise. And then turned to Elin for help."

I thought about the note I'd seen on her bookshelf. The innocent shopping list that read *HELP* that someone had passed to Elin one day. "I imagine Elin couldn't watch Mr Pesce imprison people anymore. People who had served their sentences. Rehabilitated. Ready to start their lives again, leaving past mistakes behind."

Elin shifted uncomfortably in her seat.

"So, Elin added a few more orders of fertiliser to her regular supply order, giving a bag here and there to the prisoners. Pretending it was a mistake."

Elin objected faintly. "This is preposterous. Why would I be involved with bombing anything?"

"Because all those years ago, Mr Larsen's wife died because of Evo. And Mr Pesce tore down the plans to outlaw the crops. But in the end, Evo didn't just take Mr Larsen's wife. They took your best friend."

Elin's mouth wavered. And after years of holding it together, she sobbed once loudly. Tears leaked down her face.

Mr Larsen grabbed her hand, gripping her fingers tight. *"Oh, Elin,"*

She covered her mouth with her hand as she whispered, "No one was meant to be there tonight,"

"I know, Elin. I wondered why it seemed the people putting out the fire arrived so fast. Because everyone was *already there.* Because you tried to call it off. But when you arrived, Jon and Mr Farrell were already at the warehouse. And the prisoners couldn't disarm the bomb without being seen by the cameras."

"I didn't mean for anyone to get hurt," she whispered.

"I know, Elin. But we're fine,"

"I'm so sorry," she said to us, tears pouring down her face.

"The thing is," I said, leaning forward. "We might be able to help you."

Mr Larsen set his mug down on the coffee table. "And we might be able to help *you.*"

And I looked at Mila, and she leaned forward, listening intently.

"You need to get messages offworld, right? To your network of people who can't eat Evo products. Well, we've got a ship. We can transport things to other systems if you need it done discreetly."

Mr Larsen tugged at his beard. "There is something that we need to do discreetly. But we didn't think it was possible until now." He placed his hot chocolate on the coffee table and leaned in close. "We've received word that there's an Evo defector that has some files they think would be useful to us. We obviously can't get to the meet because we can't get offworld easily. But you can. And it might be a chance for you to find out from someone who has access to the inner works of Evo to find out what they really have on you. And if they can find your sister."

"Okay," Mila said. "We're in."

The *Scout* shook as we surged into the sky. The engine roared. The ship was shaking violently as we flew through the clouds. I clung onto the armrest as Mila focused on the sky ahead of us. While I couldn't see it, I knew that Birumu - and wheat fields as far as the eye could see - were shrinking below us.

"I will be happy if I never see an electrosphere in my lifetime again," Mila called through the headset.

"Really?" I said, "I thought it was kind of beautiful."

The ship burst through the clouds, and in a moment, we entered space. Stars were scattered across the sky between blue and red planets. Golden galaxies swirled in the distance, and shooting stars dashed behind suns.

"This is my favourite sky," she said, sitting back and sighing and switching on the autopilot.

I unstrapped from the seat and folded down the dining table.

Right at this moment, as the electrosphere window opened, a software upgrade was being shipped down to the planet to install in the security bot on Pesce's farm. Once the bot received the update, it would realise the date and that the sentences of many of the workers were completed. There would be a flood of freed workers on the planet. Mr Larsen was preparing our old room for a few of them to stay with him.

"Do you have that thing for Mr Larsen?" I asked. She tossed me a data drive from her pocket. I caught it and inserted it into the tablet.

I sat at the table and loaded the video message from the townspeople who had recorded it. It was full of video statements about Mr Pesce's use of the workers, the tasia and how he'd prevented the security bot from getting its updates. Many of the prisoners had ended their sentences years ago and should not have their sentences extended. Once they recovered from the drug, they could either choose to leave or stay and work - *and* get paid for their labour.

"So, it's going to the prison board, right?" I said, typing in the details. "Come check if I'm doing this correctly?"

In the pilot seat, I saw her angle the ship slightly towards one of the crate docking bays in orbit, one with the Evo logo emblazoned on the size. She pressed a button on her dashboard, and a small package flew out of the ship like a rocket and clung to the side of the docking bay with a little red light blinking on the side.

"What was that?" I asked.

"Oh, I'm just doing my part to help slow Evo searching for us," she winked.

She sat at the kitchen table next to me, her knee brushing against mine. I didn't move my knee. She scanned the settings on the tablet. "Yes, that looks correct. Now, just send it."

I jammed my finger on the 'send' button.

"Look at us! Fighting crime, saving the day," I grinned.

"And for our next adventure," she said, "We're covert spies,"

I rolled my eyes. "We're hardly spies!"

"What do you call it then?"

"I don't think we can be spies if we're on a beachside resort planet. You, for one, would have nowhere to hide your knife in a swimming costume."

"Oh, you'd be surprised where I can hide things," Mila winked. "Besides, I don't need a secret weapon. I've got you."

What happens next?

Start *Sapling's Depths* now...

What happens next?

What will Addi and Mila find out from the Evo defector? Will Addi have the courage share her feelings with Mila? And will they be able to escape the clutches of Evo long enough to save Bianca and the Ancient One?

Find out in the next book, *Sapling's Depths*.

Scan to grab the next book:

Did you enjoy *Sapling's Aurora*?

Did you love that ending? And what did you think about Addi and Mila's connection? And what is going to happen next?!

Share your love for *Sapling's Aurora* and tell your friends to get on board the *Scout*.

Leave a review on Storygraph, Goodreads, your socials, or wherever you bought the book.

About the authour

Spencer Rose is a writer from Sydney, Australia. She writes in the early morning, with a strong coffee or two, often at a café. When not writing, she enjoys hiking, playing video games, crafting and baking.

Visit her online at spencerrosewrites.com or on Instagram or TikTok at @spencerrosewrites.